HOLBURN

TIM JEFFREYS

Manta Press, Ltd.
www.mantapress.com

Cover Design by Martin Greaves
Cover Illustration by Paul Wilhelm Keller-Reutlingen

First Edition

Acknowledgements

With thanks to Isabel Hurtado, Martin Greaves, and Robert Pope, who worked hard on the sidelines to help me complete this book. Also, thanks to Tim McWhorter at Manta Press, Ltd.

PROLOGUE

It was getting on for four o'clock in the afternoon when the train I rode arrived at Connolly Station. Outside, I jumped in a taxi and showed the driver the address Elaine had texted to me. It was out in Ranelagh, and as I rarely ventured over to that side of the Grand Canal, I didn't trust myself to find it alone. Besides, I'd been travelling for fourteen hours straight, so I was in no mood to delay myself further.

My mobile phone started buzzing after I climbed into the taxi. It had been ringing throughout the morning and afternoon, always the same number — one I didn't recognize. I ignored it, just as I'd been doing all day.

The journey from Heathrow had been a blur. I'd had a taxi drive me to Victoria, then sleepwalked my way onto a train that took me all the way to Liverpool Lime Street Station. I'd forgotten how grim the north of England could be, and what I saw out of the train window did nothing to dispel the funk I'd been in for the past few days. That low mood was unlike me, and I was surprised by my inability to shake it off. I was Gael Drake, after all, everybody's favourite drinking buddy. Gael Drake, always ready with a quip and a funny story, always available for whatever shenanigans might be afoot.

Since I'd been away from home for three months, I'd hoped the sights and sounds of Dublin would boost my spirits. But night began to fall as the taxi steered a path through the congested streets, so I wasn't able to see much. It had all turned to silhouettes, a shadow-show playing out against a blanket of washed-out blue. I could have been anywhere, in any city.

A few days earlier I'd spoken to my manager who had promised me some session work with a brother/sister duo tipped to be the new Corrs, and as much as I loved working in a recording studio, even this news hadn't given me a boost. That hole I was in, that I'd been in for days since realising the tour was coming to an end; I had some idea of its cause. It was mostly guilt. Elaine had called me half-way through the tour to tell me she was moving out of the flat we shared. At that point, I hadn't called her for a couple of weeks. I'd been meaning to, but hadn't got around to it. The tour manager had quit after the first month, and I'd stepped in as a temporary replacement.

Can you imagine how busy I've been? I told Elaine when I finally got around to calling her, or words to that effect. Elaine told me she'd had enough. I was unreliable, she said, a fucking arsehole to boot, and I spent my life running away from my responsibilities.

I had to admit; she was right.

The previous summer I'd bundled my little sister, Ava, off to a boarding school on Fannin Island because I hadn't wanted to deal with her. Also, I couldn't stop thinking about my parents' fatal car accident two years earlier, wondering: had Dad driven off that cliff on purpose? Had he no longer been able to live with the madness that followed my mother around? I was wracked with shame that I hadn't called home more, visited. Maybe Dad had needed someone to talk to. Someone who understood.

So there I was back in Dublin, but in no mood for a party. Throughout the entire journey home, I had tried to convince myself that Elaine had sent me her new address because she wanted me to visit her in order to patch things up; but I had no reason to be certain of that. My gut told me I'd lost her, that I'd pushed her patience too far this time. In truth, she'd been a saint to put up with me, and my family, for six whole years. None of my previous girlfriends had lasted longer than twelve months. One whiff of anything otherworldly and they'd be gone.

All Elaine had said in her message, apart from giving me her new address, was: *Come and see me when you get home. Please.* Nothing else. No emojis. Not even a kiss.

After what felt like an age spent idling at an endless series of traffic lights, time I spent fidgeting, watching the meter tick, and trying to ignore the anxiety building in me, we broke out of the city and entered a leafy residential area where I could see even less out of the car window. Eventually, the taxi pulled up half way along a poorly lit street of tall, three-story terraces. As I climbed out, I felt a cold churn of nerves low down in my gut, and wondered why I was getting myself into such a state.

I checked the address on my phone again, just to be certain I was in the right place. All I really wanted was to go back to the flat, shower, and sleep, but I thought it best to show Elaine she was my first priority on arriving back in Dublin. I glanced up at the house in front of me, squinting to make out the number on the door. This was it. I slung my bag over one shoulder, grabbed my guitar from the back seat of the taxi, and began climbing the steps. Halfway up, I was surprised by a security light. I couldn't help imagining how I'd look to Elaine under that harsh glare. Three months touring around Europe with a Black Sabbath tribute band, and all the fun and frolics that entailed, had left me gaunt and grey. Adding in the early flight from Denmark to Heathrow plus the subsequent hours I'd spent travelling in order to get there, I didn't need a mirror to tell me I looked like shit.

At the door, there were several buzzers for the various flats inside the house. I rang the ground-floor flat buzzer, then waited. That anxiety coiled up inside me again. I was acutely aware of the genuine possibility that I was about to make a fantastic fool of myself. Or maybe I'd be lucky and find she wasn't home. *I went to your place straight from the station*, I imagined myself telling her at some later hook-up. *Went straight there, to that house you're living in up on the hill. But you weren't there.*

I was about to ring the buzzer a second time when I heard footsteps approaching the door from the other side. To my shame, I glanced behind me, wondering if it was too late to make a run for it.

The door opened and there she stood. I was surprised at the effect seeing her again had on me. And at how different she looked. I couldn't put my finger on why at first, but later I realised it was simply that she looked happy.

She stood and blinked at me.

"Gael?"

"Hey," I said. "You sent up the bat signal, and here I am." When she looked confused by this, I cursed myself: *Idiot. Did I think I was bloody Batman now? Christ.*

She reached forward, took hold of one of my hands, and held it. "Gael. I'm so glad you're back." She stepped forward from the doorway and embraced me.

For a second or two, I didn't know where to put my hands. Then I laid them on her back and held her. It felt good. The ache inside me soothed momentarily.

Releasing me, she stepped back into the doorway.

"I didn't think you'd be this pleased to see me," I said.

"Of course, I am. Now I finally get a chance to explain things."

"Uh... explain things?"

There was the sound of feet in the hallway behind her, then a man appeared at her shoulder. He was tall and broad, with short fair hair, sharp inquisitive eyes, and hair on his chin: a goatee beard, or at least some kind of attempt at one. You could see how solid he was under his clothes, how strong, how muscular. He wore little round spectacles in order, I could only assume, to let the world know there was an intellectual hiding behind the beefcake. He was Arnold Schwarzenegger and Albert Einstein rolled in to one, and I hated him instantly. This feeling only intensified when he slid one hand across Elaine's back.

"Who is it, Els?" he said.

There was some kind of accent, possibly German, but all I could think was: *Els? Fucking Els? Since when did anyone call you Els?*

"It's that friend of mine I told you about," Elaine said, still smiling at me, her eyes holding mine. "Gael Drake."

My heart plummeted down to my feet.

Friend? Was that all I was?

I saw a look of recognition on the man's face, then he came forward, dazzling me with a set of perfect teeth and offering out his hand. He was one of those morons who thought the firmer your handshake was, the more of a man you were.

"Easy there, mate," I said as he set about trying to crush my left hand to pulp and splinters, "that's my guitar strumming hand."

He laughed as if I was joking and said, "Ah yes, you are

a rock guitar player. I am Miklos. Pleased to meet you."

"Likewise," I said, hoping he picked up the note of sarcasm I put into it. "Miklos, that's…"

"Hungarian."

"Ah. I was going to say Greek. Like the sculptures."

He laughed again and batted me on the shoulder. I don't think I could have hated him more than I did at that moment. I shot a glance to Elaine, hoping to convey that I hadn't travelled hundreds of miles to be roughed up by this meathead. Her face showed apology. She turned to Schwarzenegger.

"Perhaps Gael and I should have a moment alone," she told him. "I haven't fully explained why it was I asked him to come."

There it was. She asked. She fucking asked.

"Yes," I said.

Noticing the sharp edge to my voice, Elaine's eyes widened. I knew I was being unfair. After all, it was me who had gone off on tour and not called her for weeks. I shot a look at Miklos. *Don't be a bastard, Gael,* I told myself. *Don't.* But there was a tsunami of disappointment washing over me, and I couldn't hold back. "I just spent fifteen hours on the road," I said, facing Elaine again, "so some kind of explanation about what the hell I'm doing here would be nice, yes, thank you very much."

She looked stung. "I didn't ask for you to come straight here. Look, why don't you come in."

"No," I said, turning away from her. The thought of having to go inside that space she shared with another man sickened me. "Not now. Right now, I need sleep. I need to get my head down. It's been a hell of a long journey."

A pause. "Gael… why are you being like this?"

"Like what?"

"You're being hostile. And childish."

"Hostile?" I laughed under my breath. But when her expression showed bafflement, I had to turn away. "I'm tired, that's all. Look, this was a bad idea. You're right; I shouldn't have come straight here. I'm going to head home. We can talk in the morning. Or whenever. If that's what you want. Okay?"

Elaine's expression turned stony. "Fine," she said. "Have it your way."

I retreated down the steps and ducked into the near-dark at the end of the path, where I breathed easier. The taxi was long gone, so I started walking. It took me an hour to find my way out of Ranelagh and back to the city centre. To top things off, the heavens opened. A long walk in the rain was the perfect ending to that long, exhausting journey home. When I was halfway there, my mobile phone started ringing again.

I didn't answer it.

Back at the flat, I dried off and consoled myself with a bottle of whiskey I'd stashed in my overnight bag, then passed out on the living room sofa. I woke to needles of sunlight and a relentless pounding which I initially thought was inside my head. It took me a few minutes to realise someone was knocking on the front door.

"Just a minute," I yelled. I wasn't about to face anyone in my current state, so got up and groped my way to the bathroom. The pounding on the door started again whilst I was in there, so I only had time to take a piss and throw water on my face before stumbling to the door and opening it.

Elaine stood on the other side. This was an Elaine I was more familiar with than the sunnier one I'd encountered the previous evening. Her face was full of confrontation, and by the look of her, she'd dressed for battle in a smart pant suit under which she wore a white shirt buttoned all the way up to her throat. Her hair was tied up in a long plat which she could have used to whip me about the face had she so desired.

"Why so early?" I said, for want of anything better.

"It's gone noon."

"That's early for us rock 'n' rollers."

She shot me a look full of pity and contempt. "Can I come in?"

"It's still your place too, isn't it?"

I stood back to allow her entrance into the flat. Before she faced me, she cast her eyes around the place, and I saw her taking in the untouched pile of post behind the front door and the empty bottle on the living room floor.

"I know it must have been a shock for you, Gael," she said. "Last night, I mean."

"Goliath, you mean? Don't waste time, do you? Where did he spring from, anyway?"

"His name's Miklos."

"Looks more like a Goliath to me."

She drew a deep breath. "He's an old boyfriend. I knew him years ago, long before I met you. We kept in touch. When I told him I was leaving you, he invited me to stay with him for a while."

"To see if you could rekindle things?"

"I suppose he's always carried a torch. He's asked me to marry him."

This news had me staggering backwards. "Fuck *me*. And you didn't think to mention that?"

"What?"

"That you're getting married."

"I never said I was—"

"Funny, he doesn't look your type."

"What does that mean? He's a very sweet man."

"Sweet?"

"He is." Halting, she grabbed the sleeve of my shirt and forced me to face her. "Wait a minute. Are you jealous? Is that it? You act like you don't care about me for months, then you get all jealous when you see me with someone else."

"I do care. I've always cared."

"Really?" She shifted her eyes to the window. "You've been so distant. Even before you went off on tour. All that trouble we had with Ava, after you brought her back from America..."

"Leave Ava out of it."

"How can I? Your brother's been calling, by the way." She pointed at the landline phone, which sat in a corner of the room. It had a flashing red light to show there were new voicemail messages. "He must have called a hundred times. He wants to know where Ava is."

"Of course he does. You didn't tell him anything, did you?"

"I told him it's nothing to do with me anymore." She took a deep breath. "Gael, listen. I didn't know if you... if you still loved me. I just didn't know."

"Didn't you? Really? Isn't that how you knew you could summon me?"

Anger tightened her features. "That's ridiculous. I didn't *summon* you."

"Rattle off a text to old Gael and he'll come a-running."

"Is that what you think of me? I wanted your help. Who

else could I turn to?"

"Help with what? Picking out a wedding dress?"

Anger flashed across her face. She drew a deep breath, then looking into my eyes said: "Gael, there's... there's something haunting me."

"Haunting you?" I laughed. "It's usually places that are haunted, Elaine, not people."

"I think it was Ava. I think she found something here. Remember how we used to hear her talking to herself? Well, I don't think she was. I think she found something here. She was lonely. She didn't know how to make friends with people."

I stared at her, confused by this change of topic. "What are you talking about? Ava was only here for a couple of weeks."

"I've been seeing things. Hearing things. First here, then at Miklos' place. I think Ava found something here. Then when you scooted her off to that school, it must've attached itself to me."

I waved a dismissive hand. "You're imagining things."

"It's not my imagination," she shot back at me. "Do you think I'd come to you for help after everything if I thought I was just imagining things?"

That hurt. "And what about Goliath? Can't he sort it out?"

"Stop calling him that. His name's Miklos. You need to bring Ava back, Gael, and you need to make her get rid of this thing that's following me around."

"Did you say yes?"

"What?" She gave me a sideways glance. There was something in that glance; something that told me if we'd ever had a chance at reconciliation, it was now gone. Forever. "Is that the only thing you care about? I'm trying to tell you what's happening to me, what I'm going through because of your bloody little sister, and all you want to talk about is *him*."

"Did you?"

She closed her eyes and was silent for a long moment. "I'm still thinking about it, if you must know."

"So you're not sure?"

"I thought I was. Until last night."

"Last night?"

"Gael, don't."

"Come on, Elaine, he's not your type."

She narrowed her eyes at me. "How would you know?"

"I know you."

"No, you don't. You don't know me at all."

I tried to take her in my arms, but she backed away. She straightened out her jacket and skirt as I watched.

"I have to get back to work," she said.

My eyes followed her as she moved towards the door. "Why did you really come here, Elaine?"

She paused, her hand on the handle of the door. "I wanted to try to explain things. I didn't want you angry at me for leaving. Maybe it was a lot to ask. But if you could understand, Gael, how scared I've been living here all by myself while you've been away. The things I've seen. You never should have brought Ava here. It's not natural, the way she is. There's something very… Why didn't you just leave her in America with Carl?"

"You know why. Because she deserves a normal life, not to be a part of some freak show."

She shook her head. "She'll never have a normal life, Gael. Did your mother have a normal life? That was what I was trying to tell you when I called you two months ago." She cast her eyes around the flat. "Ava did something when she was here. There was something here, and it… it followed me. I thought I could leave it behind, but it followed. And I thought you'd want to help me. Seeing as she's your sister…" She met my eyes. "It's over between us, Gael. I mean that. I can't handle all that… that *stuff*. Your mother… and Ava. I want a fresh start. That's what Miklos is offering me. He's an engineer. He can always find work. He's been travelling from place to place ever since he left Hungary. He says we can go anywhere we want to. Live anywhere."

"And that's what you want?"

She sighed. "What I want," she said, still holding my gaze, "is not to feel afraid anymore."

My mobile phone, which I'd set down on the TV cabinet, started to buzz. Elaine looked at it.

"Are you going to get that?"

"No," I said.

"Gael?"

"What?"

"Someone's trying to get in touch with you."

"So what?"

Sighing, she reached out and picked up the phone.

"Don't," I said. "Leave it."

But she had it to her ear.

"Yes," she said. She listened for a minute or so. A look of shock appeared on her face. "Oh I see," she said. Then, "Yes, I'll put him on." She held the phone out to me.

"Who is it?"

"Holburn."

"Hol who?"

"*Holburn*. Holburn Academy. That school you packed your sister off to."

"What do they want?"

She grimaced and her eyes flashed. "They want to speak to you, Gael. They say a woman's been killed. And Ava… Ava's missing."

I squeezed my eyes shut. "Ah fuck."

CHAPTER 1

Though the two priests and I had crossed to the island separately, albeit it aboard the same ferry, we arrived as a group at the school gate. This confused the small owlish woman in the school office, and I had to spend some minutes explaining to her that I was not with the priests. Although they, like me, claimed to have been summoned to Holburn Academy by the aged school principal, Vanessa Inkson, I went there with the express intention of finding my sister, who I'd been informed had gone missing from the school four days earlier along with another pupil. What those two priests were doing there, I had no idea at that point.

"Ah, you're Mr. Drake," the woman in the school office said. "Ava Drake's brother."

"Yes," I said. "Hallelujah."

My mood had worsened since the previous day's phone call. I hadn't slept much, and I was still brooding about the situation with Elaine.

"We spent three days trying to contact you, Mr. Drake," the woman said. Though her voice remained light, she managed to convey with her expression how ashamed I ought to be of myself.

"I know," I said. "I've been away."

The woman told the three of us — the priests and me — to wait in the foyer and said someone would be along shortly to greet us.

The priests muttered between themselves as we waited, the older of the two passing between his hands a thin sliver cylindrical flask which I guessed to contain either whiskey or holy water. They were an odd couple. The older, a small slight man, had a bald crown, a short white beard and an angry fixed expression, which made me think he might bite if provoked. The younger priest I estimated to be somewhere in his thirties, although he looked younger. He was tall, round-faced, and as sweet-looking as one of Raphael's cherubs.

"So," I asked, by way of an ice-breaker, "which bit of the Old Testament did you fellas spring out of?"

The older priest snarled at me. I decided he probably was a biter, showed him my palms with apology, and stayed silent. I focused my attention on a map of the school grounds affixed to one wall until Vanessa Inkson, or 'Miss Inkson' as she insisted on being called despite her advanced years, at last arrived to greet us. She had another woman in tow, much younger than her.

Shortly after this, we were ushered together through the corridors and shown the body; something neither I nor the priests, judging by the look on their faces, were expecting or prepared for. It was being stored in the gymnasium since, as Miss Inkson made a point of telling us a number of times, there simply was nowhere else to put it. It made sense, she told us in her prim, matter-of-fact way, since the gymnasium was in the coldest wing of the building.

"All the girls here say so. All of them complain when they have to do games, especially at this time of year. Obviously, games are off the curriculum for as long as we've got *this* in here. They couldn't be happier, of course. I'm only thankful it's not summertime."

I couldn't help but make a mental a note that she'd said

this last twice already, once before we entered the gymnasium as she stood fumbling with a large set of keys, and again after she'd got the door open and led the way inside. Maybe it was her way of excusing the rank smell of decay which already filled the large space. Underneath her brusque, business-like manner, I detected a note of embarrassment at having nowhere else to store the body. Death clearly hadn't been accounted for at the prestigious Holburn Academy School for Girls.

I also noted how Inkson referred to the body as *this*, as if the deceased had become an object of inconvenience rather than a person the moment they had stopped breathing; like a car burned-out and abandoned in the school's driveway.

The body was laid out on a bench at the furthest end of the room. As we approached it, the air became more dense. The younger of the two women who'd met us at reception, the one who'd remained silent except for a straight-faced hello when the principal introduced her as 'my assistant Miss Hendy', hung back by the open doors. It was Inkson who walked with us into the gymnasium, but she wouldn't, I noticed, approach the body. I thought I understood why when the old priest lifted the sheet to reveal the head and shoulders of the dead woman. I saw how he concealed his shock by closing his eyes and taking in a small, sharp breath. The dead woman's head was locked at an unnatural angle, but worse than this was the look frozen on her face. It was a look of absolute terror. I turned my eyes away, noticing at the same time the younger priest do the same. Searching for something neutral to look at, I fixed my gaze on a jumble of hockey sticks propped against one wall. In my peripheral vision, I saw the old priest glance up, half-smiling, looking for a reaction from his companion.

"What do you say, Father Stewart?" He spoke with a

thick Scots accent.

The young priest cleared his throat and threw a glance at the body. "Looks like a broken neck, Father."

"What could have caused that, do you think?"

"Perhaps… a fall. Or a blow."

"Have to have been a powerful blow. And her face? What could account for the expression on her face?"

Father Stewart swallowed, flicking his eyes towards the dead woman. "I… I couldn't account for that, Father. Not at the moment."

The old priest let his smile broaden. "Good," he said, and — to the relief of both the young priest and myself — he let the sheet fall back into place.

I looked around for the school principal.

"Remind me again," I said, "what this dead woman has to do with my sister."

"Remind you? Why, Mr Drake — that's the music teacher, Miss Fisher, under there."

"And?"

"Miss Fisher and Ava had been at loggerheads since the start of the term. Ava had become quite unruly in her classes. We wrote to you about it, remember?"

I pictured the three months' worth of mail still piled-up on the floor behind the door of my Dublin flat. Fearing final demands, I'd left it untouched.

"Are you sure? I don't recall—"

"Ava's behaviour," the principal went on, "had become absolutely unacceptable."

I tried to align this idea with the quiet, sullen Ava I'd known; a kid so internalised that even I had given up trying to communicate with her during those few weeks when she'd stayed with Elaine and me after I brought her back from

America. I couldn't.

"So what?"

"And now the poor woman's dead."

"Ah… surely you're not implying that it was my sister who killed this woman?"

"No," the principal said. "I'm not saying *that*. Not exactly."

I glanced at the two priests. Both looked as confused as I was.

"I'm surprised she's been here so long," the younger priest said. He gestured at the body. "Like this, I mean."

"Well, it wasn't *my* doing," Inkson said. "The police were only here for a day, then they went back to the mainland. Said they'd return to begin an investigation. I pleaded with them to take the body with them, but they said it would have to stay here for the time being. Why, I don't know. I was on the 'phone for hours yesterday speaking to this official and that official, getting passed around from pillar to post, and all they did was ask *me* questions. Finally they said they'd send a water ambulance out to get her but then for the past two days the sea's been so rough that nothing's been coming over from the mainland except the occasional ferry and they won't let me put her on that. Said they wouldn't want to risk anything happening to the body. I ask you — what could happen?"

"Well, we made it over on the ferry this morning, ma'am," I said. "And I can tell you that anyone who rides that at the moment does so at their own peril. It's stormy out there. You should've seen the relief on the father here's face when we finally reached the island."

The younger priest glanced away when I caught his eye.

"But you made it," Inkson said, turning her head and frowning at the young priest. "But they won't risk it with *her*, and she's already dead. The police were supposed to be back here today, to start a search for the missing girls, but so far all we've had is you three. And meanwhile, *that* just lies there and rots. It'll take months to get rid of the smell."

I didn't doubt this last. My first instinct on entering the gymnasium had been to cover my nose and mouth with a hand. Seeing, though, that the priests did nothing but frown at the smell, I kept my hands by my sides. I'd be damned if I was going to let some bible thumpers stomach something I couldn't.

"And what about those missing girls?" I said.

We left the school, Inkson and Miss Hendy leading the way across the walled-in grounds. A hard rain fell. Before stepping outside, each of the women had acquired a large umbrella. I pulled up the hood of my jacket, for all the good that did me. The rain didn't seem to bother either of the priests, neither of whom conceeded to it. No doubt, they welcomed it as some kind of mortification. We walked a paved path across the length of the lawn. I stopped once to glance back, imagining faces at the darkened windows of the school though I saw none. Where were all those gifted girls the sign in the entrance hall spoke of? Inkson had said, shortly after our arrival, that all the girls were 'at their books'; and I'd wondered if this meant they were all in class, or if they'd been sent somewhere for quiet study.

The school building was a red-brick, turreted Gothic-Revival nightmare that had to be at least a hundred and fifty years old. The one other time I'd visited it, when I'd taken Ava there the previous summer, I hadn't noticed, or maybe hadn't wanted to notice, how creepy the place was. Maybe it was the overcast sky and general air of wintery gloom, but seeing it anew, I wondered what the hell I'd been thinking dumping my little sister in a place like that. Ava, of all people.

At the end of the paved path we arrived at a high cast iron gate which was set into the wall. Miss Hendy went ahead, lifting the latch on the gate and opening it. I caught her eyes as I passed through. She was — I guessed — in her early thirties, although she dressed older. Her large, heavily lashed brown eyes gave a solemnity to her face and hinted at some southern-European blood: Spanish or Italian. Her dark hair was drawn roughly back and knotted behind her head. She gave me only a polite half-smile and bowed her head a little, avoiding my gaze.

"That gate is never locked?" I said to the principal.

"No. It doesn't have to be. Our girls never come down here. They wouldn't."

"Wouldn't? Why so sure?"

"I know them; that's why. Not one of them would *ever* come down here. Especially after... recent events."

The grass beyond the gate was overgrown. I saw at once that ahead of us was the vast area of woodland I'd earlier noted on a plan of the school that was mounted on the wall near the main entrance. The ground underfoot was boggy, and the women picked their way carefully as they led the way towards the trees.

I spoke to the principal. "You said that Ava was seen leaving the grounds through that gate back there on the day she disappeared?"

"That's right. It was Miss Hendy herself who saw her."

I glanced at the younger woman.

"It was sometime after lunch," Miss Hendy said, as though startled by the attention. "I was getting some of the girls in from the lawn and I saw Ava and another girl walking together towards the far wall. Arm in arm, they were. I assumed they wanted some time to be... to be alone. I didn't think for a minute they were going to leave the grounds. Miss Devonshire-Bartram... I mean, Lucy — her of all people, I assumed she never would've set foot outside the gate. After what happened. Everyone knows not to..."

I stopped walking and stared at Miss Hendy. "Knows?"

She glanced away, then back at me. "Not to leave the grounds. Especially Lucy."

"Especially?"

"We have strict rules here, Mr Drake," put in the principal. "No girl leaves the grounds unaccompanied. No one steps outside the gates after dark. We don't need locks and bolts to enforce our rules. They are simply *understood*."

"I see." My attention remained with Miss Hendy. "And who is this Lucy?"

"She..." Miss Hendy began, but Inkson cut her off.

"A star pupil. Came here on a scholarship, as I recall. Her parents weren't the wealthiest, but she would not let that hold her back. We all knew she would do well here. Despite her background. Smart girl. She excelled at everything. Popular and always so sweet to the other girls. And, of course, she was developing into quite a... looker. A quiet girl though. Kept herself to herself. That's probably why she bonded so well with Ava. She inspired some envy in a few of the other girls. And, perhaps also because of her station in life, there was a bit of bullying, swiftly stamped out I might add. Initially, we were all pleased to see that she'd made a friend."

"She and Ava were friends?" I said, ignoring Inkson and continuing to address the younger woman.

"They were… some people thought..."

"Best of friends," Inkson said. "Nothing more."

Now I gave the principle my attention. "And was Ava bullied here too?"

Inkson pursed her lips. "We don't tolerate that kind of behaviour here at Holburn, Mr Drake. It was all dealt with quickly, I assure you."

"So she was bullied?"

Inkson flashed her eyes at me. "Stamped out. Very, very quickly."

Before I could say anything more, she waved at Miss Hendy and continued on towards the trees. At the outskirts of the wood, the women stopped and would not venture further. A little way in among the trees, someone had strung yellow police tape between a few trunks, cordoning off a small area. One line of the tape had snapped. The wind toyed with the loose ends.

"This is where we found poor Miss Fisher, just inside the trees."

I followed the two priests as they walked to the cordoned off area. The women remained at the outskirts of the trees. The branches offered some shelter from the rain, but it was gloomier beneath them.

"Flat ground," the older priest said, stepping inside the cordon. "No way to account for that fall. Not here."

His companion said, "It didn't have to be a fall that killed her, Father."

I laughed. "What are you two? Dog-collar detectives?"

The older priest snarled at me again. "We have to investigate if we're to do the job properly."

"Job? What job? Why exactly are you here for?"

Instead of answering, the old priest strode past me, searching the ground with his eyes. Thinking he might find some sign of Ava, I followed him. He'd only gone a short distance when he raised his head and looked deeper into the wood.

"Will you be venturing in, young man? To look for your sister?"

A chill found me and I shivered. "These woods could go on for miles," I said. "We don't know for sure that she went deeper in."

"But we have to do something? Don't we?"

"I suspect she'll come out on her own. When she's ready. Can't stay in there forever."

I gave the old priest a dark look then turned to walk out of the wood. When I emerged from the trees, I saw Father Stewart speaking to the two women. Beyond them, by the gate through which we'd left the house, I noticed a dark-haired figure dressed in black. In the same moment in which I noticed the figure, it had vanished, ducked away out of sight, perhaps; but I was sure it had been a young woman about Ava's age. She had stood watching us. I thought she might've been wearing a school uniform, but with no coat or umbrella to shield her from the pelting rain.

Strange, I thought. I made a mental note to ask, later, about this person.

Clearly keen to escape the rain, Miss Inkson hurried ahead of the others through the gate into the school grounds and along the path to the house. She didn't wait for the rest of us or even glance back to see if we were following. Miss Hendy was more considerate. Though she too dashed up the path through the grounds, she waited for the priests and I by the door of the school and held it open so we could enter. She had her shoulders hunched like someone anticipating a blow and wet strands of hair were stuck to her brow. As I passed her, I glanced into her face again and saw that she was looking toward the end of the garden in the direction of the woods. Her expression showed, in that unguarded moment, concern.

Re-entering the house I found the older priest standing in the hallway chatting with the principal. He turned and addressed his companion, who walked behind me.

"Miss Inkson has kindly agreed to show us the rooms where the two missing girls slept. I want you to take a good look around. Make notes if you have to."

"Certainly," Father Stewart said. He reached inside his jacket and took a small notepad and pencil from the breast pocket of his jacket.

"Jesus Christ," I said. "He's Pope John Paul and Miss Marple all rolled into one."

Inkson shot me a look of undisguised contempt then shifted her attention to the older priest.

"Tell him to be careful what he writes," she said. "You're here to investigate a death, not poke around in the private affairs of the school. Our patrons expect a certain *silence* when it comes to matters of their children's education. There's our reputation to think of. I won't have anything staining that. Holburn Academy is considered one of the most outstanding learning environments in the entire world. It would not do to have our doors thrown open to the glare of the outside world."

"Shouldn't these investigations be left to the police?" I said.

The older priest gave me the same look I'd just received from Inkson. "From what we've been told, the police'll be of no use in these particular circumstances." Before I could ask him what he meant, he turned to Inkson who had begun leading us towards the stairs. "I assure you, we're only interested in matters pertaining to the supernatural. Whatever your gifted girls get up to here in pursuit of their individual educations is no concern of ours."

"Wait a minute," I said. "Supernatural?"

There was no answer. The group moved ahead of me, so that I had to hurry to catch up. We were climbing the wide, richly carpeted stairs. Miss Inkson led the way, still chattering about the school and how it must have its privacy. It sounded almost as if she had something to hide, but I thought instead that her insistence was more her way of demonstrating her own importance and the responsibility of her position. I had already surmised that she had very little else going on in her life. To all intents and purposes, she *was* the school.

As we reached a turn in the staircase, there was a riot of footsteps from the floor above before girls of various ages, all dressed in grey uniforms, flooded the stairway. They bowed their heads when they saw Miss Inkson and clutched their books to their chests; but some shot quick glances and little coy smiles at me as they passed. For a few moments they surrounded our group, halting our progress up the stairs, but then they were just as quickly gone. Inkson clapped her hands at the stragglers, saying: "To your next class please, girls. Hurry up."

One lingered to glare at me. She was about Ava's age — that is, fifteen or so. She was thin-faced, horsey-looking you might say, with long straight light brown hair, and a large birthmark on her left cheek. The look she gave me could have curdled milk.

The dormitory where Ava and Lucy had slept, along with eight other girls, was at the top of the house. Miss Inkson explained that the attic had been converted before the school increased its intake the previous year. On reaching the dormitory, Father Stewart began pacing the floor, casting his eyes around, moving along the line of beds and occasionally picking up some object from a night-table and examining it. He opened wardrobes and passed his fingers over the hanging clothes.

"What exactly is Velma looking for?" I said to the older priest.

"Father Stewart is looking for evidence of supernatural phenomena," he said without looking at me.

"So that's it? That what you two are here for, is it? A ghost hunt?"

"We came to free the school from some unquiet presences, yes."

"You mean an exorcism? You came to do an exorcism."

He locked eyes with me. "Miss Inkson thinks it was your sister, Ava, who disturbed these spirits, who conjured them up to terrorise the school. Is that right, ma'am?"

I raised my eyebrows and looked at Inkson for

confirmation, but she merely bowed her head. It was the first time I'd seen her show humility. "Well, there have been quite a series of unexplained events here lately. We're at our wits end. At this point we're willing to try anything. Anything."

"And... what? You think Ava was somehow responsible for these *unexplained events*?"

"She..."

"She controlled them somehow."

It was Miss Hendy who spoke. I looked at her, as did Inkson and the priests and she appeared to wilt under our scrutiny.

"That's... that's what some of the other girls say. We had to re-situate the others who slept here. They refused to share a room with Ava."

"That's ridiculous," I said, and perhaps Miss Hendy noticed that my tone lacked conviction as she raised her head and narrowed her eyes at me as if to say: *You know about this?* Despite myself, I felt the heat of a blush. Putting my back to the others, I shifted towards a tall narrow window set at about waist height in the opposite wall. Pushing the window open, I looked out across the school grounds. The heavy rain still fell. Water ran off the roof and made a splattering sound on the paved yard some distance below. A chill entered through the gap I'd created. I remembered the dead woman we'd been shown in the gymnasium, the music teacher whose name I couldn't recall, and how her head had been tilted to the side in that unnatural way. Then I remembered the flat ground of the woods where the body had been found.

Fall could've been from this very window, I thought. *But then what? Someone dragged the body to that spot in the woods where she was found?*

I closed the window and turned back into the room,

thinking to make a note of this thought somewhere, do my own detective work, but I met the eyes of Inkson and paused. She was pinning me with a cold expectant stare. I decided to wait until later to jot down my speculations.

I glanced back towards the window. "I saw someone. Not now, but earlier. When we were standing at the edge of the woods, near where the body was found. I saw a girl watching us from inside the school grounds." I looked at Inkson again. "Do you know who that might've been? A pupil? A member of the staff, perhaps?"

Mrs Inkson appeared flustered for a moment. "At that time, all the girls were at their books, and the staff were busy supervising them. You must have imagined it."

"No," I said. "I don't think so."

"Are we about done here?" Inkson said, turning the collection of keys in her hands.

I wasn't done. "Then you don't know who this person was?"

"There wasn't a person there. *I* didn't see anyone." She held my gaze. "There's one more thing I wanted to mention, Mr Drake. We were contacted by your brother a few days ago, and we were obliged to inform him about your sister's disappearance."

A flash of anger must have shown on my face as Inkson blinked and drew back as if she thought I might strike out at her.

"I thought I'd made it clear that my brother was not to know of Ava's whereabouts."

"Mr Drake, it is not our duty to withhold information from our pupil's surviving family members. Especially in the circumstances." She was recovering her composure, and her expression changed to one of insinuation. "We had no idea

Ava was related to Carl Drake. The Spirit Whisperer. Isn't that what he calls himself?"

I felt the priests' eyes fix on me, though I didn't dare look their way.

"He's a phoney," I said. "Take it from me, it's all nonsense."

"Still," Inkson went on, "perhaps he can explain some of what's been happened here when he arrives. A man of his experience."

"He has no experience. I told you it's all..." My thoughts went dead. "When he arrives? What do you mean? He's coming here?"

"He was in America when we spoke, on tour I believe, but he said he'd fly back immediately to help search for Ava."

"Like fuck!"

The old principal reeled as if slapped.

"You had no fucking right! I want that man kept the hell away from my sister, do you understand me? I'm her legal guardian. Carl's just a... he just wants..."

Miss Hendy stepped forward and took hold of my arm. "Mr Drake," she said in a calm but sure voice. "Perhaps you should take a moment to compose yourself."

CHAPTER 2

Alone and still fuming, I sought the rooms in the school basement which Inkson had described as the family rooms. They were the rooms where visitors slept. They had given me a key with a plastic tag on which was inscribed the number 29. I struggled to find the correct door as I ducked along the basement corridor. Pipes ran the length of the ceiling and I had to bow my head to avoid striking it on one of them. When I eventually found room 29 and got the door open, I was less than enthusiastic about spending the night there. The room had only a small single bed pushed against one wall, and opposite this was a child's wooden desk. There was no window, and the room had a thick musty smell. My sinuses reacted as soon as I stepped inside. When I stood by the desk, I noticed it was covered with a thick layer of dust. I moved one finger through the dust, leaving an O shape on the surface.

"Filthy."

I couldn't help but wonder if Inkson had chosen this room for me as some kind of punishment. I would have to find Ava fast, I decided, and get to the bottom of what was going on. I didn't want to be spending too many nights in that airless little room. Dumping my shoulder bag by the door, I sat down on the bed and ran my fingers through my hair, thinking about my brother Carl. One of the main reasons I'd enrolled Ava at that school was to keep Carl away from her. And I'd thought she was well hidden. How could he have found out? Had Elaine said something to him after all? Or perhaps Ava herself had contacted him. Perhaps she actually wanted to be dragged back into that ridiculous sideshow he called his career. Perhaps he had enticed her somehow. It was only a matter of time, after all, before his whole charade collapsed without Ava. Spirit Whisperer — ha! If only people knew the truth.

I told myself I had to find Ava before he arrived. I had to find her and make her disappear again; somewhere he would never think to look, somewhere she could live a normal life.

I remembered what Elaine had said.

She'll never have a normal life, Gael. Did your mother have a normal life?

My stomach growled, and I remembered that I'd bought a sandwich from a kiosk on the mainland harbour. I'd meant the sandwich to be my breakfast, but the ferry crossing had played havoc with my stomach and I hadn't been able to think about eating. It would do for now though. As I lifted myself and reached towards my bag, a sudden bolt of shock when through me as I was certain I saw the bag shift a little on its own towards me.

"What the…?"

It happened again. The bag jerked across the floor towards me of its own accord.

I stood up and backed up against the wall, looking into all corners of the room. I looked at the bag again and blinked. Had it moved? Had it moved, or had I imagined it? Tentatively, I put my hand out towards it and again it slid a few inches across the floor towards me. With a gasp, I pressed myself against the wall, looking frantically around the room. On instinct, my hand went to my throat and touched the crystal quartz pendant I always wore, the one my mother gave me when I was a teenager, the one she said would protect me from what she described as 'bad energies'.

"Is someone here?" I said aloud.

There was no response. Nothing in the room moved. I could feel the thud of my heartbeat. I swallowed.

"Who is it? Who's here?"

I waited. Suddenly my bag slid all the way across the floor and halted at my feet. A cold bolt of fear shot through me, and I gave a yelp and leapt to one side. Aware then of my own harsh breathing, I waited for something else to happen. Nothing did.

"Is someone there?" I said again. Then I remembered my notebook. Crouching and unzipping my bag, I rummaged inside until I found the pad. There was a pen jammed into the spiral. My hands trembled the whole time, and the hairs on the back of my neck bristled. I laid the pad open on the little desk and placed the pen down next to it, then backed up into my corner again.

"Who... who are you?"

I stared at the pad and pen, picturing the pen rising and some invisible hand using it to spell out a name on the pad. That didn't happen.

"Who are you?" I said again. "Do you have a name?"

I began speaking the alphabet out loud, something I'd seen Carl do in a theatre somewhere, years ago. There would be some kind of knock or thump or a table set up on the stage would shake when he got to a certain letter. Then he'd begin again until he had all the letters to spell out a name. I made it to Z without a response of any kind, so I started over.

"A... B... C..."

I listened for a knock or a tremble but there was nothing. I decided to address whatever was there directly.

"Who's here?" I said, noticing the quaver in my voice. I cleared my throat. "Are... are you a pupil here at the school? I mean... were you a pupil?"

Nothing.

"If you were a pupil here, how long ago?"

No response.

"Did Ava bring you back here?"

Silence.

"Why are you here?" I asked of the empty room. "What do you want?"

Again, there was no response. I let out my breath. I hadn't realised how much tension I'd been holding in my body. As I released it, I slid my back down the wall until I was in a crouched position. I was still shaking, but I began to doubt what I'd seen. I was tired after all. Dog-tired, hungry, and hallucinating. Was it possible I'd imagined seeing my bag slide across the floor of its own accord? Hearing footsteps outside the room, I raised my head. There were voices too as the footsteps passed on the other side of the door.

"All that time stuck in the seminary and your first assignment is to a girl's school. That must be like a dream come true for you, lad."

"Father?"

"You'll need all your training if you want to sneak one past that old baggage of a headmistress though. She doesn't want us here, nosing around, and I can't say I blame her."

A pause.

"You think she's hiding something? That there's something she doesn't want us to know?"

"Oh, there's a lot she doesn't want us to know. Some of it might even be relevant."

The voices faded with the footsteps as the priests

continued along the basement corridor. Inkson must have assigned them rooms down here in the basement too. I was glad to know I wasn't the only one to be shown such discourtesy.

I glanced at my watch. It was only four o'clock, but I knew outside it would already be dark.

"Ava," I said, thinking of my sister out there somewhere in those woods. "What the hell have you done, girl?"

Inkson had told me I could eat in the school refectory, but not until six o'clock when all the pupils had left. I found the implication that I was some kind of threat laughable and insulting, and noted that she didn't ask the same of the priests. They wore dog-collars so they could wander the school freely, but they viewed me as some kind of hot-blooded lothario who would be unable to control himself around the girls here. I'd wanted to tell her that schoolgirls weren't to my taste. For a moment, I'd even thought it would be amusing to tell her that I preferred the older lady. *Much older*, I imagined myself saying before giving her a wink to send her scuttling back to her office. In the end I said nothing and decided to toe the line for however long I was here. It was looking like my sister had already caused enough trouble for the two of us.

It meant I had a couple of hours to kill and I didn't much feel like spending it in that airless room, especially now I suspected there was a presence there. But I didn't know where else I could go, so I sat back on the bed and tried to call Elaine on my mobile. Though she'd told me to my face that it was over between us, I refused to let go of the possibility that she still felt something for me. But I couldn't get a signal. I got a few bars out in the corridor but there was no connection. It was quite possible, of course, that Elaine had blocked my number. I managed to get through to the Dublin recording studio where I was supposed to be laying down some guitar work. But no one was picking up and so I left a message on the answerphone telling them not to expect me for a few more days at least. I knew it was pointless. Tony, my manager, had probably brought in another session guy to replace me already, and most likely I was off the following year's tour as well. *You're an excellent player, Gael,* he'd said when I told him I'd be skipping town for a while. *You've got something special. But there are a lot of excellent players out there, and some of them are reliable with it.*

But what else could I do? I had to sort this mess out. I had to find my sister.

After giving up on the phone, I lay on the bed and somehow managed to doze off for an hour or so. At six I freshened up in the little shower room across the corridor then headed upstairs to find the refectory. All I'd had to eat that day was that one sandwich and my stomach growled.

The refectory, when I found it, had the look and sense of being recently busy with people, but it was unoccupied. The chairs at the long tables were haphazardly arranged, and remnants of food, napkins and plastic cups littered the floor and tabletops. There was a buffet bar fronting a kitchen on one side of the room, so I went there and helped myself to as much of what remained as I could fit on a plate. A few minutes into my meal, I heard someone enter through the doors behind me and approach my table. It was Miss Hendy. Her hair was no longer knotted up behind her head. She now wore it down, which suited her better as it was thick and luxurious. I nodded to her.

"Mr Drake," she said. "Can we talk?"

I shrugged, munched a broccoli floret into extinction then said, "Call me Gael if you like. What'll I call you?"

She hesitated then said, "I suppose you could call me Audrey."

"Audrey? Okay. That works."

She showed a momentary confusion. "Listen, Mr... Gael, I think we should start a search for Ava and Lucy tomorrow. If you're happy the two of us can go. I'm not worried so much about Ava — she can look after herself, she's a resourceful girl as I'm sure you're aware. Lucy's the one I'm really concerned about."

"What was it you wanted to say earlier? Are those two having some kind of love affair? I didn't know Ava liked girls."

"I think she..."

"Say it."

"I think she likes anyone who can get through to her."

"That sounds like Ava."

"They always said they were a gang."

"A gang? Two can't be a gang."

Audrey looked down at her hands, which were clasped on the table in front of her. "I don't know if it was a love affair, but I'm afraid Lucy became quite besotted with Ava. She worshiped her. I think she'd do anything Ava asked. That's why I'm worried. She might not be thinking straight. Ava could..."

"Was Ava really such a menace?"

"She became very unruly, yes. Angry."

I nodded. "She didn't want to be here?"

"It didn't seem like she did. It seemed like she wanted to punish the entire school."

"And that music teacher. The dead one. Did Ava really have a hand in that?"

Audrey pressed a fist to her mouth and shut her eyes. "I don't know. I don't know." She drew a deep breath and opened her eyes again. She took a folded sheet of paper from inside her jacket and laid it out on the table. It was a map of some kind, though not a modern one. It was hand drawn.

"What's that?"

"It's an old map of the island from the late 1800s. Back then, the school building was a stately home. In the woods there's an old stone lodge that was once part of the house. I think that's where Ava and Lucy are. If we can find the lodge, I'm certain, we can find them." She placed her finger on the map at the centre of the woodland behind the school. Though there was a building at the centre, I saw at once that no paths or markers led the way to it.

"I suppose we can try."

"We'll set off early, before the pupils are up and about, so we can make the most of the daylight."

I felt that implied threat again, as if I was some child-gobbling wolfman.

"Shouldn't someone keep an eye on the priests?"

"Keep an eye on them?"

"You know you can't trust their type around children."

Audrey's eyes widened. "The school principal will know where they are at all times."

Seeing how sincerely shocked she was, I relented. "It's okay, I'm only messing with you." I gave her my best wolfman grin.

"What've you got against the priests?" she said.

"Ah. I had more than enough of their type hanging around the house when I was a kid. Enough for a lifetime. Always bothering my poor old ma." I slapped a hand down on the map by way of changing the subject. "Tomorrow then. I'm game. I doubt I'm going to sleep much in that stuffy little room you've stuck me in down in the basement, so the earlier the better, as far as I'm concerned."

"Yes," Audrey said, uncertainly, looking at me with her head titled to the side.

We both stood.

"Very well, Mr Drake," she said.

"Gael."

With the dark, the rain slackened. Leaving the refectory, and finding the halls quiet, I took a detour and exited the school by the same back door Miss Inkson had led the priests and I through earlier. I used the light of my mobile phone to pick my way along the paved path and out again through the gate at the end of the garden. The dark was fuller there under the trees. I trudged through mud and dead leaves, my light skittering about between the trunks and the ground ahead of me. At one point my foot disturbed something and there was a thin, womanly shriek which scared me half to death. Seeing something on the ground moving, I directed my light downwards.

"Jesus. A fucking toad."

Who knew toads could make a noise like that? I was shaken, but I walked on a little way into the wood. My heart beat fast. When I'd gone about as far as I felt comfortable going into those trees, I stopped and called out:

"Ava!"

There was no response. I called out again:

"Ava! Lucy! Are you there?"

I turned my head to the side, listening intently, but there was no answer. What had I been hoping? That Ava might emerge from the woods if she heard my voice? That I could resolve the girls' disappearance that very night and get her away from the school before Carl turned up? That I could avoid tomorrow's trek with Miss Hendy?

Then, from somewhere close by, I heard something moving through the bracken. Swinging my light to the right, I glimpsed a figure passing through the trees before ducking out of sight.

"Wha…?"

I tried to flush this figure out with my light but couldn't. I was sure though that it had been a tall, pale man dressed in a black suit. I was about to move forward to see if I could pick up the trail again, when I heard footsteps at my back. Swinging around, I saw a girl of about fifteen or sixteen covered in a long hooded shawl. As soon as my light hit her, she turned and broke into a run, heading for the gate and the garden and presumably, the school. I called after her but she didn't stop. Shaking off my momentary surprise I gave chase. As the girl broke free of the trees, I saw others like her emerging from the wood at various points and joining together at the school gate. There might have been seven or eight of them in total. I could hear them speaking in hushed, urgent voices. What were they up to? They all wore hooded shawls and were carrying long, thin objects which I couldn't make out. I called to them, but they flung open the school gate and vanished. By the time I was inside the grounds of the school again, both the man in the black suit and the group of girls were nowhere to be seen. Since I hadn't seen them going up the steps to the rear doors, I realised they must have known some other entrance.

"Jesus," I said, bent double as I regained my breath. "What the fuck is going on in this place?"

When I got back to my room in the school's basement, the first thing I noticed when I turned on the light was that someone had been finger-writing in the dust on the desk. Underneath where I had drawn an O were these words:

MY NAME IS EVE.

I WAS A PUPIL HERE.

AVA WAS MY FRIEND.

AVA BROUGHT ME BACK.

I WANT TO HELP U FIND HER.

CHAPTER 3

The following morning was as grey and washed-out as I felt. I'd somehow managed short periods of sleep, but I'd spent most of the night tossing and turning on the narrow bed, frequently opening my eyes to stare into that total dark and wonder whether or not I was alone. I could feel a presence in the room with me, which I hoped was the Eve spirit as that at least seemed benevolent. But there was no way of knowing how many spooks and spirits Ava had dragged out of the school's brickwork. In my experience, spirits projected emotions out into the rooms they occupied, and what I felt, as I lay there in the dark, was some kind of calm, watchful presence.

Before seven I was back in the refectory with Audrey for a hasty breakfast. She was pale and silent, and dressed for the expedition in walking boots, jeans and a waterproof jacket. As I'd not planned on trekking through woodland, I had to make do with my battered leather and the shoes I'd arrived in which at least had a decent grip.

"Are you ready?" Audrey said.

She led me out of the back door and across the rear garden to the spot on the outskirts of the wood where we'd stood with Inkson and the two priests the previous day, and where I'd ventured alone the same evening.

At least today it's not raining, I thought to myself, although the woods looked as cheerless and uninviting as they had when I'd first encountered them. Audrey produced a compass from her backpack. I could see my trepidation mirrored on her face when she looked into those trees. That spot where we were standing. Wasn't it the very spot where the music teacher had been found dead? And how long had Ava been in those woods? She could have filled the whole place with spooks and sprites already.

We walked in silence for a while, with Audrey from time to time studying the compass and the map she'd shown me the day before. I let her lead, saying nothing about the pale thin man in the black suit I saw watching us from a distance between the trees. I was sure it was the same man I'd glimpsed the night before. I was also sure that he was not flesh and blood. He was not of these times. There was something pre-war in the cut of his clothes. His black hair was swept back in a widow's peak and he had a thick moustache. Whenever I saw him, he would glare back at me for a few seconds before vanishing, only to reappear in another spot deeper in the woods. I felt his presence was some kind of warning. I hoped Ava had been smart enough to be discriminate in the spirits she raised, but then I remembered the dead music teacher and I felt afraid.

"The police should be arriving back at the school today," Audrey said, as if she'd known what I'd been thinking. "About time."

I nodded, but secretly wondered if the police would let Ava off the island when — *if* — we finally found her. No doubt there'd be questions to answer.

"I want you to know," Audrey said, tugging me out of my thoughts. "That everyone did their best for Ava when she first arrived here. Myself included. I kept a close eye on her. I suppose she rather reminded me of myself at that age."

"Did she?" I waited for Audrey to elaborate. When she didn't I said, "So what's your story?"

"I was a pupil here myself once."

"Were you? And you decided to stay on?"

Audrey nodded. "I had nowhere else to go. You see, I was orphaned myself as a teenager."

I halted. "Were you?"

"Yes. My father — he... um... he took his own life when I was thirteen years old. And my mother, well, I like to think my mother died of a broken heart. She'd loved him so much. But it was anorexia. Her heart just gave up."

"Like Karen Carpenter?" I said.

When Audrey stared blankly at me, I sang a snatch of 'Close To You' before realising, too late as always, how insensitive I was being. "I'm sorry," I said. "Really. Ignore me, I'm an idiot."

She didn't disagree. We continued walking.

"I'm not trying to sell you a sob story," Audrey said. "I'm just trying to explain why I related to Ava. I felt sad for her. I know how it feels to lose your family."

"She still has family," I said. "She's got me."

She gave me a look which said all she needed to about that.

"I don't think they ever planned to have children," she said. "My parents, that is. I don't think they knew how to fit me into the life they had with each other. I don't think they needed anyone else. Not really."

"So they sent you here?"

She caught my eye and nodded. "Here is where I found a kind of family. You might think Miss Inkson's a little stuffy, but she's been almost like a mother to me. That's why I stayed on after my exams."

"Stuffy isn't the word I would've chosen."

She caught my eye again. There was the hint of a smile on her lips. "She's really not that bad."

"I'll have to take your word for that."

She laughed.

We didn't speak again until we'd been walking for a further half-hour or so. I'd stopped looking for the man in the black suit. I kept my eyes on the path ahead of us.

"So?" Audrey said. "What exactly is the problem with Ava's other brother? You got a bit upset when you found out we'd informed him about Ava's disappearance."

"He wasn't supposed to know where she was. The whole point of sending Ava here was to keep her out of his clutches."

"His clutches? That sounds a bit dramatic."

"Yeah, well. He had her working with him for a while in that crackpot show of his."

"You mean the spirit whispering thing?"

"It wasn't good for her to be caught up in all that so I took her out of it. There was a fair bit of money from my parent's will which they'd set aside for Ava's education. I think they meant university education, but I convinced the solicitors that it would be a good idea to use it to send her to this school. I knew she could pass the entrance exams, it was just a matter of making her see what was best for her."

Best for her? I thought, hearing myself say this. *Was it best for her? Or was it best for me?*

"Your parents' death..." Audrey said, "it was a car accident, wasn't it?"

"They were on holiday in the Scottish highlands. Drove right off the edge of a cliff."

"That's terrible."

"Yes. It was sad. Especially after everything Mum had

already been through with her surgery."

"Surgery? Was she ill?"

"No. Not ill exactly. She had to have her jaw reconstructed. She got kicked in the face by a horse at a pony show."

"My God. How could that happen?"

I suddenly regretted bringing the subject up and wondered how best to backtrack. "She had a bit of an odd effect on animals sometimes. Dogs used to go absolutely wild around her. It could get kind of crazy."

"How awful."

"Some people just have that weird kind of energy, you know?"

I hoped that the dismissive way I said this would throw Audrey off the scent, but my mouth had a habit of working even when I wanted it to stop. The wrong words at the wrong time had a habit of bubbling out of me. Always. It was one thing about me that had frequently exasperated Elaine. *Gael*, she would say, *would you just shut your fucking bake! Every time you open your mouth, you make everything a hundred times worse!*

I looked into Audrey's face and hoped she wouldn't voice any of the questions that were clearly percolating in her mind. When she made to speak, I quickly cut in:

"They're at peace now," I said, before foolishly adding: "At least I hope so."

Christ! Elaine's voice in my head again. *What in God's name did you say that for?*

Audrey's eyes widened. "Ava seemed very troubled when she first arrived."

"I expect she was."

"She kept to herself. She didn't seem interested in

getting to know the other girls. She ended up very isolated. She seemed lonely. This was before she became palls with Lucy. There was a period, at the beginning, where she appeared to have an imaginary friend. That's unusual for a girl of her age, and it concerned us. The girls in her dorm said they would hear her whispering to herself at night. Then the problems with Laura... I mean, Miss Fisher began."

"Miss Fisher?"

"The music teacher. The... the body we showed you..."

"Ah, *that* Miss Fisher."

Audrey seemed cautious to continue. "Ava also seemed to have an issue with me. I would pass her sometimes in the corridor and she would say things to my back."

"Things? What kind of things?"

"Unpleasant things."

"Like what?"

Audrey bit at her bottom lip. "Whore. Slut. Things like that."

I stopped walking again. "Ava said that to you?"

Audrey nodded.

"Why would she say that to you?"

"I have no idea."

"Ava doesn't talk like that. Ava's..." I was going to say 'a good girl', but I caught myself. Clearly, Ava was not the same girl I'd once known. But had I known her? Had I known her at all? She'd been a closed book when I brought her back from America.

Guilt came then. I should have looked out for Ava better. Visited her at the school, checked that she had settled in okay. I should have given her more time. If I hadn't been so wrapped up in my musical career and in my turbulent relationship with Elaine...

"Ava…" Audrey held my gaze for a long moment. "Some of the girls have said they've seen things. Heard things. Back at the school. That's why Inkson called the priests in. She thinks if they do an exorcism that'll put the girls' minds at ease. She wants to parade the priests around, do it very publicly."

"I doubt it'll do much good. The best way to get rid of a spook is to find out what's keeping it here. In this world I mean. There's usually something. They hang around. Ava just brings them more… into the foreground."

Audrey drew her head back and blinked at me. "You believe it then? That Ava has… she has these abilities?"

I glanced away then met her eyes again. I nodded.

"What about you?" I asked her. "You haven't seen anything? Heard anything? Strange…?"

"No," she said, glancing away. "Nothing."

"Ava's always been…" I shrugged. "Special."

"And you? Your brother?"

I shook my head. "Just Ava. Carl's a fraud."

"Your parents?"

"My mother."

"Good God." She stopped walking and put a hand to her brow. "You never should have brought her here."

"I'm sorry. I am. I kind of hoped she'd grow out of it once I got her away from Carl. I wanted her to have a normal life, not to be some sideshow freak. Can you understand that?"

Audrey shook her head. She looked at the map again and pointed to the left. "This way, I think." There was a blunt edge to her voice.

We walked the lip of a steep ravine, when a gust of wind moved through the trees behind us, shaking leaves from some of the lower hanging branches and stirring those that lay on the ground. I got an odd prickly sensation along my spine. Audrey turned a questioning look on me, her eyes wide as if she'd had the same feeling. She was stood on the lip of the ravine and some instinct made me reach out and grab hold of one of her arms a moment before she lurched sideways with a yelp of fear. With her free hand she clutched onto my jacket, almost dragging me down into the ravine with her, but I managed to get a firm footing on the edge and pulled her up with me instead. We stood holding onto each other for a moment, staring into each other's startled faces.

"What the hell happened?" I said. "Did you trip?"

She shook her head. "Some… something pushed me. I felt it. I felt this huge shove."

I glanced down into the ravine. "Some… *thing*?"

"I felt hands on my back. I swear. Then a push."

"There's no one here," I said, glancing around at the surrounding trees. But I could feel it then, a palpable sort of rage, something small and thwarted, like a child's anger. "There's no one here."

"I'm telling you, I felt…"

"Maybe we should head back. You're not safe here."

"*I'm* not safe."

"I should do this on my own."

She stared into my face, searching out answers to whatever questions were now circulated in her mind. "It's not all just nonsense, is it? All the spirit whispering stuff. Is it? It's Ava, isn't it? It's true what you said. She's the one who… It's her who can…"

"We should get away from the edge of this ravine, don't you think?"

She drew a sharp breath. "It's true then? Tell me. Ava's some kind of…"

"Listen, you need to get away from this fucking ravine because something wants you lying at the bottom of it, you get me?"

That got her moving. Still holding on to each other, we climbed higher until we found a flatter stretch.

"Tell me the truth," Audrey said. I tried to avoid her gaze but she wouldn't let me.

I took a deep breath. "Ava's filled this place with ghosts," I said. "They're everywhere. I've encountered two, maybe three already."

"Three? Where?"

"Here. And at the school."

"Here?" Audrey darted her eyes about the surrounding trees. "Now?"

I nodded. "It's not safe. Some might be friendly, but some — I think — aren't. I don't know what the hell Ava thinks she's playing at."

"We should go back," Audrey said. I could see the terror in her face. "Both of us."

"What? What about Ava? And the other girl?"

"We're not the right people for this. The priests should be… or the police. Someone. Not us. I'm going back. One of Ava's ghosts killed Laura Fisher. I know it. And it just tried to kill me. Push me into the ravine. Oh God."

She turned and started walking back the way we'd come. I looked the other way, the way we'd been headed, and a short distance away, in a break in the trees, I saw the man in the black suit. He was staring right back at me. Hi arms were folded behind his back. His pose, and his fixed expression, made me think of old school photographs. I could imagine him stood dead centre behind two rows of pupils. And I'd been right in what I'd thought earlier. He was a warning. His face was a warning. I knew then that I didn't want to be alone in those woods. I shouted after Audrey and ran to catch up with her.

We arrived back at the school to find that the police, as Audrey said, had finally returned.

CHAPTER 4

For the rest of the day, I did my best to lie low and avoid bumping into any of the constabulary. I knew at some point I'd be questioned, but I was determined to put it off for as long as I could while I tried to figure out what to do next. It wasn't until the following morning that they summoned me to the gymnasium where a man calling himself Detective Inspector Hadlee had a desk set up. He was a broad, blunt-faced man; crumpled and grey and weary-looking, like an old dog. He looked like he'd been in the job too long.

It was a relief to see that the body of the music teacher had at last been removed, ferried back to the mainland for burial. The stench of death and decay still hung in the air and recalled to my mind that glimpse I'd been allowed of the dead woman's face after I first arrived, something I'd since done my best to forget. All the top windows in the gym had been opened, so it was cold in there, and I could hear the steady sweep of rain across the school's courtyard. I sat and shivered whilst Hadlee scrutinised my features.

"How would you describe your sister, Ava, Mr Drake?" he eventually asked.

"Quiet. Keeps to herself."

"Were you aware of her increasingly bad behaviour since arriving at the school?"

"Not until a few days ago."

"You weren't informed?"

"Like I said, not until I arrived here."

"By all accounts, she'd been completely out of control these past few weeks."

I shrugged. "She's a teenager."

He lifted his head and held my gaze. One eye twitched, betraying the anger he tried his best to keep a lid on. "Do you think it's possible your sister could have been involved in a woman's death, Mr Drake?"

I lifted my head. "Do you?"

He drew a deep breath. "I was interested in getting your opinion, if you don't mind."

I was aware of him observing my reaction. "No," I said. "Never. Not Ava. She wouldn't harm a fly."

It seemed a long time before the man lowered his eyes. "Ava has another brother, yes? Carl Drake. *The* Carl Drake? The famous—"

"I know who he is."

"Ava used to perform with him, didn't she? Over in the U.S."

"I'm not sure perform is the right word."

"What is the right word, Mr Drake?"

I cast my eyes around the walls. "He's a con-artist. He cons people. He had her helping him do that for a while." Before he could interject, I changed tack: "Are you going to go look for my sister? She's been missing almost a week now. And the other girl…?"

"We've already done a thorough search of the school."

"And the woods. The woods *behind* the school. The girls were seen leaving by the back gate the day they disappeared."

He showed me his coffee-stained teeth. "In cases like this we tend to find that people end up returning to the place they started from without any kind of intervention. If those girls are out in those woods, how long do you think they can stay out there? In this weather? With no food or water? If they are out there, in all likelihood they'll make their way back soon enough."

"But..?"

"But... my feeling is they headed for the harbour as soon as they could and got on a ferry. We'd do better searching for them on the mainland, and indeed we already are."

"The sea was too choppy for ferries."

"A few made it across. We're looking at the CCTV."

"You mean to say you're not going into those woods?"

"No need. If the girls are in there, they'll come out. Eventually."

"But couldn't they have gotten lost? What if they're hurt... injured?"

I examined his face now, looking for an inkling of what he knew, or suspected, about what had unfolded there at the school. What was still unfolding. It seemed odd that he was so offhand about sending a search party into the woods. Was it possible his officers had already gone into the woods, only to get spooked as myself and Audrey had? That they were refusing to go back in?

He went on for a while, asking about Carl who he seemed to find fascinating. I restricted myself to yes and no answers. He finally sat back in his chair and said:

"Have you met the two priests Miss Inkson invited here? Apparently, they're here to perform an exorcism. Did you know that?"

"Yes. We travelled here together on the ferry a few days ago. Never really cared for the old God-botherers myself though."

He hesitated, staring hard at me.

"But an exorcism?"

"What about it?"

"Do you believe in ghosts, Mr Drake?"

His gaze was so direct, so unwavering, I turned my face away. What could I tell him? That there was a spirit called Eve, a former pupil at the school, occupying the room where I slept? Would I tell him about the number of times I'd woken up in that windowless place thinking I'd felt someone lie down on the bed next to me, but finding—when I switched on the light—that I was alone? Would I tell him about the man in the black suit I'd seen in the woods, his face full of reproach? Or would I tell him about my childhood? The strange people I'd sometimes encountered in our house? The odd sensations I'd had of not being alone when I knew I was? How I'd sometimes hear my mother talking, and a voice answering her, when I knew she was alone in the kitchen or her bedroom? How I'd come to accept and then ignore this behaviour until I'd noticed Ava doing the same thing?

"No, sir. No, I don't. You?"

"I like to keep an open mind."

"Well, those two priests look very Old Testament to me so whatever it is they came here to do, I'm sure they believe it's the right thing, in the circumstances."

Hadlee's eye twitched again, and I knew he'd felt my little barb. It was then that I noticed for the first time the little silver cross on a chain around his neck and I thought: *Shit*. He gave me a long look, then sat up and cleared his throat. I sensed the atmosphere between us shift, then settle. He waved his hand as if to dismiss me. I stood.

"I believe your brother is on his way," he said. "I very much look forward to meeting him."

"If I were you," I told him over my shoulder as I moved towards the exit. "I wouldn't."

On the way back to my room in the basement, I saw a huddle of girls outside a classroom door. Hearing my approach, most of them scattered. Three remained, sidling away from the door and watching me as I approached. I recognised one of them as the horsey-faced girl with the birthmark who had fixed me with a contemptuous look on the stairs the day I arrived. This time she smiled at me.

"Hey," I said.

"Hey," she returned. "I love your hair."

That stopped me in my tracks. "Yeah?"

"Yes," she said. "How do you get it to grow out of your nose like that?"

The three girls huddled together and snickered.

"Good one," I said, shooting her with one finger. Having just spent three months trapped in a tour bus with a bunch of beery rockers, I could have eviscerated her with a comeback but I decided she wasn't worth the effort. This obviously wasn't the reaction she'd hoped for. The three of them stopped sniggering and scowled at me. I nodded towards the classroom door. "What's going on in there?"

"See for yourself," Birthmark said. "Oh and good luck finding your sister."

I rounded on her. "What do you mean with that?"

She threw up her hands and made a mock-innocent face. Then she and her friends traipsed off, putting their backs to me and muttering between themselves. I stared after them for a moment.

When I turned to the door they'd been crowded around, I saw the two priests inside the classroom. The desks had been pushed against the walls, and the older priest stood in the centre of the cleared space with his arms outspread. He was reciting something in what sounded like Latin. Father Stewart took great strides in a circle around him, sprinkling what I guessed was holy water in all directions from a little silver canister. I would've laughed if I hadn't been so worried about Ava. Audrey and Miss Inkson stood side by side near the blackboard, looking on. Audrey shifted her gaze and caught my eye. There was something in her expression: anger or irritation, as if she meant to imply that what we were witnessing was all my doing. I made a gesture of apology, to which her face darkened further, so I continued on my way.

Following my chat with Detective Inspector Hadlee, an idea had formed in my mind. I had dismissed it at first, but as I watched that exorcism taking place it came back more persuasive. That idea was that I should get the hell out of that school. If Ava and Lucy whatever-her-name-was were not lost in the woods but had, as Hadlee proposed, headed for the mainland, what was the point of me hanging around that place? What was I doing there, anyway? Why did I feel so guilty about Ava? I'd done everything I could for her. I'd got her away from Carl. I'd tried to set her up there at the school. All this — the dead music teacher, the gallery of spooks — all this was her mess. I had my own life to sort out; and I had no desire for a brotherly reunion with Carl when he finally turned up.

As I stood outside that classroom, getting accusatory glances from Audrey, I decided: *to hell with all of them!*

Ducking back down the corridor, I bounded down the basement stairs and hurried to room 26. A mild elation filled me as I thought about getting out of there. If I could make it back to Dublin before nightfall, I could get myself over to the recording studio. Putting down some guitar on somebody else's record was just what I needed to take my mind off things. Maybe I could even salvage my relationship with Elaine — yes, I was still beating that dead horse — and stop her marrying that Miklos guy. Back in my basement room, after throwing my things together, I hoisted my overnight bag onto my shoulder.

"Bye, Eve," I said as I closed the door behind me. "Happy haunting."

I thought I heard a thump from behind the closed door, which made me pause.

Upstairs, I stuck my head into the school office, tossed the startled woman my room key without a word, then a few moments later I was hurrying down the front steps with a new sense of freedom that made me smile despite the rain that still fell in steady sheets. The sky gave me pause — it looked black and biblical. I couldn't see the sea from the school courtyard, but I hoped it was calm enough for ferries. In the back of my mind, as I exited through the main gates, I realised I'd been expecting someone to appear to try to stop me leaving; Miss Inkson perhaps, or Hadlee, or even one of those irritating priests. But no one did. Beyond the gates was a steep path with woodland on either side that led down to the harbour. As I descended the hill, I decided to try one more time to ring Elaine. I would tell her I was headed back to Dublin. Then, depending on her reaction to that news, I would ask her if we could meet up somewhere to talk.

I was buoyant. For the first time in weeks, I felt like

myself again.

I dialled Elaine's number and let it ring. There was a jitter of nerves in my belly.

"Come on, pick up."

There was a click and a man's voice said, "Hello."

"Hey, Miklos," I said, recognising the accent. I wondered why he was answering Elaine's phone. "How's it going? Is Elaine there?"

"Who is this?"

"It's Gael. Gael Drake. Elaine's friend. The rock guitar player. We met a few days ago, remember?"

He sighed. "Ah, Gael. I didn't recognise your voice."

"That's okay. Can I speak to Elaine, please?"

There was a long pause. Then he said, "Gael, I've got some bad news."

The second I heard those words, my good spirits sank beneath a swelling sense of dread. "What? What are you talking about? What's happened?"

Another pause. "Gael," he said. There was a hitch in his voice. "I'm sorry to tell you that Elaine has passed away."

His words hit me like a hammer blow. I stumbled to the side of the path and leaned one hand against the trunk of a tree.

"Passed away? What do you mean?"

"I mean she's dead, Gael. Elaine is dead."

A numb feeling came over me. I wiped the rain water out of my eyes. "Dead?"

"Yes. There was an accident."

"What kind of accident?"

For a long moment he didn't speak. Then, "Gael, Elaine was hit by a car on Cow's Lane yesterday. We'd... we'd gone into the centre to have a drink together and she... she started acting strange. She said there was someone following her. I tried to get her home, but she became hysterical. She just kept saying there was someone following her. There wasn't anyone. She was acting crazy. She started running. She was running all over the road screaming and… a car came… a car…it… she just…"

I didn't hear any more because at that point I hurled my mobile phone as savagely as I could down the hillside. I don't know what happened after that, only that I began screaming and shouting. I cursed Ava. Cursed myself. I kept remembering how Elaine had asked for my help when she came to see me at the flat, and how I'd dismissed what she tried to tell me and brought the conversation back to her relationship with Miklos. I saw the truth then. All this had come about because I'd tried to do the right thing by bringing Ava back from America. Because of what I'd done, two people… two people were dead.

Had I been closer to the harbour I would have thrown myself into the sea. They heard my screaming and hollering back and the school, where — as I found out later — Miss Inkson wanted to dispatch a couple of police officers to see what was going on. But Audrey had placated her and ventured out herself accompanied, for some reason, by Father Stewart. I don't remember much, except how kind and concerned they both were. Somehow the two of them managed to get me back to the school, and return me to that room I'd previously occupied in the basement. They lay me down on the bed. I was given a couple of sedatives by the school nurse and slept for eighteen hours straight.

CHAPTER 5

I dreamt I was in a windowless room with bare concrete walls. It could have been a basement room. A single lightbulb dangled on a cord from the ceiling. I stood with my back against the wall. In the centre of the room a group of maybe twenty or thirty people clustered around a small desk, like a child's classroom desk, at which sat my sister, Ava. She was hunched forward with her eyes squeezed shut and her hands pressed over her ears. There was a look of anguish on her face. The people who crowded around were all pushing and jostling each other in order to get as close to Ava as they could, and they were all shouting and pleading with her, their words intermingling into a cacophonous babble. Over the noise of all these people I could somehow hear Ava calling to me.

"Gael," she begged. "Please, Gael. Help me. Make them stop."

I tried to push my way into the throng, to reach her, but I couldn't find an opening. When I pulled one person back in order to force my way through, it proved to be Elaine. Seeing her there I understood who all those people crowding around my sister were. The dead.

"What are you all doing to Ava?" I shouted over the roar. "Why don't you leave her alone?"

"She's not natural," Elaine said to me, her voice hollowed out. "She's a freak."

"She's my sister."

"She's not right."

Ignoring her, I continued trying to push my way in among the bodies, calling to Ava: "Ava, I'm coming. Ava, I'm here."

"Gael," Ava called back. "Make them stop. Make them stop. Please. Make them leave me alone."

"Ava!"

The scene changed, and I saw myself at seventeen years old, sat on the sofa in the front room of my parents' house in Galway. It was the day Mum brought a newborn Ava home from the hospital. She had placed the swaddled baby into my arms, and I'd held her, this tiny new life, this fragile thing. My sister. Right then, I'd made a silent vow to be her protector. I didn't know if she could even see me, but her eyes held mine. They were an opaque blue. I couldn't shift my gaze away from hers. There seemed to be some understanding which passed between us. I felt she knew who I was and what I had vowed. But then, in the dream, I heard a thudding noise. I looked up and saw faces crowding at the window. It was them again. The pale anguished faces of the dead. The doorbell rang, repeatedly, and the letterbox flapped and fists pounded on the door. I looked down at baby Ava and her tiny mouth opened and she said, "Gael, make them stop. Make them stop."

At this point I started awake. The lamp on the cabinet beside the bed had been left on. I had a moment of serenity, of relief at surfacing from those dreams of my sister, before the memory of Elaine's death returned and there seemed to be no air in that stuffy little room. I sat up, panic taking hold of me, gasping, feeling that I couldn't breathe. Since I wore the same clothes I'd worn the previous day, I got up off the bed and pulled on my shoes. I struggled with the door for a few moments, before realising it was unlocked.

As I rushed along the corridor towards the staircase, I struck my head on a pipe that ran along the ceiling. Despite the pain, I didn't pause. I rushed up the stairs to the first-floor corridor, where the air felt so different it was as if I'd been submerged under water. I leaned against the wall as I recovered myself. As I felt calmer, I saw a dark-haired man of about my age, dressed in a tan-coloured suit, walking towards me leading a line of girls a few of whom stopped to goggle at me. He had the kind of effortless good looks that brought out the cynic in me, the kind of looks guys like him cruised through life on. They didn't need witty banter or guitar-playing chops to impress the ladies, they just rolled out of bed, combed a hand through their hair, and had women falling at their feet.

"S'il vous plaît," the man called to the stragglers, ushering them back in to line. Before departing, he turned to me and gave me a long look of pure unadulterated hostility and contempt.

"Tête de nœud," I muttered, an insult an old girlfriend of mine from Bordeaux had cursed me with so many times it was etched on my memory. The man gave no indication of having heard me, but I was pleased to notice a few of the girls smirking behind their hands.

A clock on the corridor wall told me it was almost nine-thirty, so I thought it would be safe to head to the refectory for some breakfast. I was about to set off that way, when a noise from straight ahead caught my attention. Further along the corridor a swing door opened and closed repeatedly. I gazed at the door for a moment, trying to work out what was causing it to swing. Another set of swing doors beyond it were closed, so there was no chance of a draft. And there was no one around but myself. When I made a move towards the doors, they stopped swinging, but now it was the next set of doors that were in motion.

It took me a moment to realise that I was being led. But by who? Could this be Eve? A prickle of disquiet ran through me, but having a sudden sense that there was something I needed to see, I walked on. After the second set of doors, the papers on a notice board fluttered as if a hand had moved through them. I saw ahead of me the doors that led out onto the lawn behind the school. Reaching the doors, I put my face to the glass panels and saw the iron gate at the end of the lawn spring open of its own accord.

I didn't want to go out there. I had no way of knowing if it was the Eve spirit who led me. My feelings of foreboding weren't helped by the fact that whoever or whatever it was seemed intent on leading me to the edge of those woods where the body of the music teacher had been found. I backed away from the door, but then I saw the gate slam shut and crank open again so violently, it was a wonder it didn't fly off its hinges.

"Okay," I said, and wondered who I was talking to. "Okay. You win."

I pushed out through the door and began following the paved path across the lawn. The day was overcast, and a squally wind raced the length of the walls like a loosed dog looking for escape. Briefly, I thought I saw a dark-haired girl dressed in school uniform and a black coat stood at the end of the lawn, by the gate. But I blinked, and this vision vanished. I hurried down the path. Arriving at the gate, I at once saw a pale blonde-haired girl stood at the edge of the trees looking back at me. She too wore the school-uniform, but it was snagged and torn. Her hair was dishevelled and her face and hands were scratched and grimy. I at first took her for another of Ava's ghosts, but then she reached out a hand towards me and said, "Help. Help me."

I ran the remaining distance and caught her in my arms as she fainted.

Sensing another presence, I looked in among the trees and saw the pale man in the black suit about twenty meters away, stood between two tree trunks and staring back at me. Shivering with dread, I turned away from him and began hurrying back towards the school with the girl in my arms. I saw now that she had an ugly bruise across one cheekbone, and a cut above one eye. Her lips were dry and cracked. There was a damp, earthly smell coming off her. Her eyes flickered open again as I made my way back up the paving-stone path through the lawn.

"Are you Lucy?" I asked her. "Are you Lucy...?" I couldn't remember the surname, only that it was double-barrelled.

She gave the slightest nod of her head.

"My name is Gael Drake. I'm Ava's brother."

Her eyes focused on me for a moment.

"Where is Ava, Lucy? Where is she?"

She lifted one hand and motioned toward the woods. "Ava's..."

"Is Ava still out there? Is she out there in the woods somewhere?"

Her lips parted. But then her eyes closed again, and I felt her slump in my arms.

Before I'd crossed the lawn, Miss Inkson came rushing down the stone steps leading up to the school entrance as fast as her little legs could carry her. After glancing at the unconscious girl in my arms, she put herself in my path, preventing me from climbing the steps.

"Not that way," she said. "There's a side entrance. Take her in through the side entrance."

"For God's sake, this girl needs medical attention."

She looked me in the eye, letting me know who was in charge. "I don't want gossip, Mr Drake. We must avoid a scandal at all costs."

"You've had two priests performing an exorcism in a classroom back there and you're worried about gossip."

"And who's fault is that?" she said, still holding my gaze.

I had to look away. "All right — the side entrance. Where is it?"

She led the way. I followed the trot of her heels, the girl so heavy in my arms I couldn't wait to set her down.

Inkson glanced over her shoulder. "Did she say anything?"

"Not much. Just told me her name."

Inkson halted, studying the girl's face. "Whatever can have happened to her?"

"I don't know. But I'm going in there to find Ava. I can't wait any longer. Look at the state this girl's in. Something must have happened to them. Something bad."

Inkson said nothing, only examined my face. I thought about the man in the black suit I'd encountered each time I'd ventured into the woods. I knew I was going to have to get past him if I wanted to find Ava, and the thought chilled me.

Around the side of the building was a trade entrance which opened onto the kitchens beside the refectory. There, a few people were preparing lunch. They paused to stare at us. One woman in white overalls opened her mouth to say something, but after one look at Inkson's face she closed it again.

"Is there a doctor on site?" I asked.

"We've only a school nurse. Miss Keen."

I recalled a tall thin red-haired woman who had handed me two pills the previous day before I sank into oblivion.

The little nursing station was close to the refectory, so we managed to get Lucy there without anyone else seeing us. Miss Keen had me lay Lucy out on an examination table. I told her how I'd found her at the fringe of the trees behind the back gate, how she'd spoken before fainting into my arms. I didn't mention that I'd been led out the back way by doors swinging of their own accord and unseen hands ruffling papers on a noticeboard. In fact, I'd forgotten myself that it was the banging doors and the fluttering noticeboard papers that had led me to the girl.

"Where are you going now?" Inkson said when I moved towards the exit.

"I'm going to find Ava. But first I need to get a hold of those priests."

Ignoring whatever she was about to say next, I went back to the refectory kitchens and told the woman in overalls that I needed supplies for a trek. Her face was full of query, but I could see she daren't ask any questions. She gave me a bottle of water, chocolate, and some hastily made sandwiches. She even gave me a little backpack to put it all in. I thanked her and raced out to look for the priests. By good fortune, I met them in the corridor. Father Stewart asked how I was.

"Fine," I said.

"I'm so sorry for your loss."

I pushed away the memory of what Miklos had told me the previous day. There was no time to grieve. I would deal with that later.

"I need your help," I said to the priests. "Both of you."

The older priest gave me a disdainful look. If he wouldn't help me, I felt sure Father Stewart would.

"You two," I said. My bluntness took them by surprise. I was glad about this. "Come with me. I've another little ceremony for you to perform out in the woods."

"What're you talking about, man?" the older one said.

"What's your name, Father? We were never properly introduced."

"You can call me Father Bannister."

"Well, Father Bannister, there's a spook out in the woods I need you to get rid of for me."

"Get rid of?"

"Yes, that thing you do." I mimed sprinkling holy water.

"What makes you think there's something out there?"

"I've seen it."

He narrowed his eyes. "Seen it?"

"Yes, I've seen it. Is there an echo in here? He's in my way."

I started walking towards the back door, hoping they were intrigued enough to follow.

"Mr Drake, are you serious?" Father Stewart said.

"Deadly."

"You got your Bibles? Your holy water? All that stuff?"

"Mr Drake…"

I kept walking, glancing back once to check they were following. They were, if a little uncertainly.

"Come on," I said. I hurried out of the back door, down the steps, and took the path across the lawn at a sprint. The priests came after me, a flap of vestments. In no time we stood at the edge of the woods. The priests picked their way gingerly across the boggy ground.

"What are we doing out here?" Father Bannister

demanded.

"Performing an exorcism. That's what you're here for, isn't it?" I walked in among the trees, peering deeper into the woods. "Where are you?" I said under my breath. "Come on, where are you?"

Father Stewart caught my eye. He must have picked up some sense of how serious I was, and he looked scared.

"What's out here?"

"I told you, a man. Dressed in 1900's get up."

"And you're certain this is some kind of… presence?"

I laughed. "Oh, he's got presence all right."

"But…"

"We need to go further in. Then he'll show himself."

The priests appeared reluctant. Father Stewart looked terrified, and Father Bannister glowered at me as if he still thought I was yanking his chain.

"Come on," I said, and curiosity got the better of them and they followed.

We trudged through the trees for a while and encountered nothing and no one.

"This is some kind of joke," Father Bannister said at last. "We'll not wade about in the mud after this fool all day, Father Stewart. Come on; let's head back to the school."

"Wait," I said, but they'd already put their backs to me and began returning the way we'd come. They'd only gone a few paces when they halted at the sound of someone approaching. Father Stewart might even have given a little yelp. All I could do was freeze and listen to the footsteps getting closer. The priests were twisting the caps off their little canisters of holy water. Then I spied a figure through the trees, and told them, "Wait."

"Gael," said a female voice.

"Over here."

She stepped into view and I noticed the two priests visibly relax. "It's Miss Hendy," Father Stewart said as if to assure himself. "It's only Miss Hendy."

Audrey came forward, looking at each of us in turn, at our startled faces, as if we'd lost our minds.

"What's going on? What're you all doing out here?"

I had opened my mouth to answer, but then I felt a shift in the atmosphere, as if the world had suddenly darkened and my gaze moved beyond Audrey and I saw him. He stood stock-still a short distance behind her between two trees, glaring back at me.

"There," I said. I reached out and grabbed Audrey's wrist, pulling her to me. With my other arm I gestured at the priests. "There! There he is! Do it! Do what you do!"

They looked around the clearing. I knew they must have felt it, even if they hadn't seen him, that tilt in the atmosphere. Then Father Bannister saw what I was pointing at, and his eyes narrowed. He froze for a moment like a dog that had spied a squirrel. Then he nudged Father Stewart and the two of them set to work.

"What's going on?" Audrey said. She too had looked in the direction I'd been pointing, but I turned her around to face me instead.

"Never mind." When I began walking her away from the scene, the man in the black suit appeared up ahead. I grabbed Father Stewart's sleeve and span him around.

"Over there! Over there now!"

Both priests were murmuring in Latin and flinging holy water about the clearing. They sprinkled some over themselves, and then threw some over Audrey and I, starling us so that Audrey let out a little scream. The priests crossed themselves. When I looked again the man in the black suit had vanished from the spot where he'd been, and I thought they might have succeeded in dispelling him, but then I felt that by now familiar chill, glanced to the side and saw him stood there, closer than before.

"Over there now!"

Audrey caught sight of the spook then and screamed again. I held on to her.

"It's OK," I said.

An icy rain came then, surprising me, surprising all of us, slashing hard through the leaves of the trees. The rain fell so hard it blinded me. I had to turn my face to the ground. Audrey screamed again. Father Bannister began shouting, in English this time. The sound of the rain was so loud I only caught some words.

"Save me, O God, by thy name… oppressors seek after my soul… God is mine helper… cut them off in thine truth…"

I had a sense of something circling us, drawing closer. There was a sudden noise that rang loud through the woods, like a bellow crossed with an animal growl. I squeezed my eyes closed and held onto Audrey. Now, beyond the sound of the hard-falling rain, both priests were shouting, their voices becoming one, compelling our spirit friend to be in peace.

"He himself commands thee, who has ordered those cast down from the heights of heaven to the depths of the earth. He commands thee, he who commanded the sea, the winds, and the tempests."

That odd bellow sounded again. I felt something pull hard at my shoulder, almost wrenching me backwards, into what I don't know. I would have gone had Audrey not clutched me around the waist when she felt the pull. The priests went on shouting and gesticulating in an odd little frenzy.

"Why dost thou stand and resist, when thou knowest that Christ the Lord will destroy thy strength? Fear him who was immolated in Isaac, sold in Joseph, slain in the lamb, crucified in man, and then was triumphant over hell."

That strange angry bellowing sound seemed as if it were responding to them. Defying them. Roaring back at them.

Something yanked at my shoulder again, tearing me out of Audrey's arms and throwing me to the ground. I spat as my face was forced into dead leaves. As I tried to clamber to my feet, some invisible force pushed me down again.

There was silence. Audrey and the priests stood looking at me with their mouth hanging open.

"Get on with it!" I yelled at the priests.

This shook them out of their trance, and they continued on with their ritual.

"I exorcize thee, most vile spirit, the very embodiment of our enemy, the entire spectre, the entire legion, in the name of Jesus Christ."

Audrey too had come to her senses and hurried forward to help me to my feet.

Then the rain let off just as quickly as it had begun. I stood shivering, drenched through to my underwear, listening to the priest's booming, commanding voices.

"I exorcize thee, most vile spirit. Save me, O God, by thy name, and judge me by thy strength. Judge me by thy strength. I exorcize thee, most vile spirit. I exorcize thee!"

To my surprise then, Audrey too began shouting, pitching her voice above the priests.

"Ernest Hoare Hales," she said. She gave me an uncertain look then continued. "Those girls got out. That day of the fire, those girls you went back in to save got out. They got out on their own! Everyone got out! You don't need to be here anymore! Everyone got out!"

I stared at her. What the hell was this?

Seeing me watching her, she fell silent, throwing out her arms in a hopeless gesture.

After a moment, I realised the priests were silent as well. Sunlight was breaking through the branches overhead. It might have been this that created a sense of calm. All was quiet. But it wasn't that. I could no longer feel the man in the black suit, no longer feel his dark presence. Wiping rainwater out of my eyes, I looked at the priests.

"You did it," I said. "You fucking did it."

They looked as stunned as I was. Father Stewart's lips moved.

But had they done it? I looked at Audrey.

She pushed away from me. Her hair hung in wet clumps across her forehead. Her blouse was plastered to her skin. She gave me a savage look.

"Do you mind telling me what the... what the hell's going on? What you're all doing out here?"

"You know what's going on. You saw him, didn't you? And what was all that stuff you were shouting? Something about a fire? Everyone got out?"

"I..." Her face softened. She noticed the pack on my back.

"You're going to find her? Ava?"

I nodded.

"I'll go with you."

I shook my head. "No. Just me this time."

The clearing darkened, and I glanced up to see that clouds had once more blocked the sun. At the same time, that sudden calm that had descended vanished again, and I felt the atmosphere once more infused with an angry presence.

I looked into Audrey's face. "He's still here."

"What?"

"It didn't work. He's still…"

I turned to the two priests who stood facing me and saw their eyes were fixed on something behind me. Reeling around I saw a small dark figure, just a silhouette, stood at the edge of the clearing. I noticed it only for a split second, then I was distracted by a loud cracking sound and looking up I saw a large branch lurch downwards as it split from one of the trees overhead. The branch was directly above Audrey and to my eye it looked heavy enough to kill her. I opened my mouth to cry out, to warn her, but Father Stewart must have registered the same thing I did, in the same moment, and with a cry he leapt forward and pushed Audrey out of the way of the falling branch. However his heroism placed him under the branch instead, and as Audrey fell sideways, it struck him a terrible blow across the top of the head and carried him with it to the ground.

There followed an awful moment of stillness.

I ran to Father Stewart who was trapped beneath the fallen branch. His mouth was open and his eyes bulged, but I knew he was dead, knew that he had to have been killed instantly, even before I pressed a couple of fingers to his neck to check for a pulse. Father Bannister crouched beside me and tugged at his companion's dog collar and the buttons at his throat. He began shaking the younger priest's shoulders.

Gently I touched the crown of Father Stewart's head and my fingers came up thick with blood.

"Let's get this off him," I said.

Together, Father Bannister and I lifted and set aside the heavy branch that pinned Father Stewart to the ground. Falling to his knees, Father Bannister crouched again over the younger priest and began shouting into his face.

"Father Stewart. Father. Father Stew… Andrew! Andrew!"

"It's no use. He's dead, Father. The branch hit him square across the head. No one could have survived that."

Glancing up, I caught Audrey's eye. She had got back to her feet and stood at a distance, watching us, one hand pressed to her mouth. I looked around the clearing, but saw no sign of the small dark figure.

"That was meant for me, wasn't it?" Audrey said, shifting her gaze to the fallen tree branch. "I was supposed to be the one who…"

"He saved your life," I said.

She squeezed her eyes shut in anguish. Tears fell across her cheeks.

Father Bannister continued trying to rouse his companion, slapping his face and shaking him.

"It's no use," I said, standing. "He's dead. Can't you see he's dead?"

"Dead?" Father Bannister rose to his feet, his face full of fury. His mouth worked then his eyes narrowed as they fixed on me. "This is your fault, Drake!"

"Listen…"

"You brought us out here! You did this!"

As he came at me, I moved towards Audrey, but she backed away from the two of us, moving away in the direction of the school.

"I'm going to get the police," she said.

"Audrey, wait…"

She shook her head. "No, Gael. I'm going to get the police."

She turned and ran. I looked back at Father Bannister, who stood glaring at me with his fists clenched at his sides. His face was flushed, and he took deep, gasping breaths. I looked beyond him to the prone body of Father Stewart and I felt a surge of guilt. Did I do this? Was his death my fault? Another one. Dead because of me. Either way, I knew that one way or another I would be the one to answer for it.

CHAPTER 6

Father Bannister, Audrey, and I sat in plastic chairs outside the gym like errant schoolkids waiting to see the headmaster. None of us having been given the opportunity to change, we sat and shivered in our rain-drenched clothes. One after another they summoned us inside to be questioned by Detective Inspector Hadlee. Father Bannister went first. He had sunk into a state of silent shock, his face still flushed, his eyes staring into nothing, so I doubt Hadlee got much out of him. Audrey went next. She emerged about twenty minutes later, her face set, and left without so much as a glance my way. Then one of Hadlee's constables waved at me from the gymnasium door.

Hadlee welcomed me from behind the same desk he'd sat at for our previous interview. Beyond him, laid out on a bench, was a body covered with a white sheet. But it was not Miss Fisher. I knew this had to be Father Stewart. I thought about how kind Father Stewart had been to me the previous day, after I'd received the news about Elaine. It occurred to me, also, that the way things were going, that gym would never give up its stench of death.

"What were you doing out in the woods today, Mr Drake?" Hadlee asked when I took the seat opposite him.

"Exorcising a ghost."

He gave me a low look. "What were you really doing?"

"What do you think I'd be doing out in the woods with a couple of priests?" I said. "Playing croquet?"

Hadlee leaned across his desk and stared at me until I squirmed and felt a blush rise to my face. I had to look away. He was clearly a practised intimidator. My quips wouldn't have any effect him.

"Mr Drake, why do you feel compelled to make jokes all the time? A man is dead. The bodies seem to be mounting up thick and fast around this school."

"Yes, I've noticed. What can I tell you? A tree branch fell on his head. Or do you suspect foul play?"

He drew back. Chewed at his bottom lip. "We've no reason to suspect foul play. Not at the moment. Tree branch broke off and struck him across the head, by all accounts. Freak accident." He narrowed his eyes, saying in a softer tone. "I do know there's something else going on here, though, Mr Drake, and trust me when I tell you that I will get to the bottom of it."

"Why don't you get to the bottom of it by going out into those woods and finding my sister? I found Lucy whatever-her-name-is this morning at the edge of the trees. That means she and Ava didn't head for the harbour and catch a ferry over to the mainland. That means Ava's still somewhere in those woods."

"We'll be mounting a search in due course, Mr Drake."

"In due course?"

He nodded.

"Can I go now?"

He sat up. "No, you can't. I'm not finished with you yet."

He continued questioning me for a while and seemed annoyed that I stuck to my story. That is, the truth. I had no way of knowing what Audrey and Father Bannister had told him, if anything, but I suspected that they too would have told the truth. I could tell by the way Hadlee affected a casual air that he secretly waited for me to say something that didn't match what he'd got from the other two. That he was daring me to tell a lie.

Leaving the gymnasium, I went straight to the school office and asked where I might find Miss Hendy. I was directed to another office further along the corridor. There was no answer to my knock. I knocked again and after a moment the door opened and Audrey glared out at me. She'd changed her clothes and now wore a black turtle-neck sweater with black trousers, as if she was in mourning. She'd obviously been crying again. Her eyes were red-rimmed and her face pale and washed-out.

"What is it?" she said.

"Are you okay, Audrey?"

"What do you want, Gael?"

"I wanted to check you were okay, that's all. It wasn't your fault, what happened to Father Stewart."

She gasped and began to close the door. I put my arm out to stop her.

"So," I said, "all that stuff you were shouting out in the woods. Want to tell me about it?"

She looked hard into my eyes, and something in her expression softened. "I have a confession to make," she said.

"Want me to fetch Father Bannister."

A smile touched the corners of her mouth. "No."

"What is it, Audrey?"

She hesitated then said, "I've seen him before. That man in the black suit."

"Have you?"

"Yes, a few times. I'm sorry I didn't tell you when we were walking in the woods. When you asked if I'd seen anything strange... any ghosts, remember? I wanted to say something, but I was hoping I might have imagined it. I didn't want to believe it. I didn't want to believe that there could be ghosts. But here, look at this."

Beckoning me inside the small office, she closed the door. Then she went to the desk and opened one of the drawers. From it she took what looked like a large black photograph album.

"What've you got there?"

"It's a collection of old photographs put together from when Holburn first opened in 1902 up to the 1940s. I borrowed it from the school achieves."

Laying the album out on the desk and opening it, she pointed at a black-and-white photo on the first page. It showed a group of men arranged in three rows outside the school entrance. They were all stern looking, and dressed in black suits and gowns. Audrey pointed to a man in the centre of the middle row. Unlike the others, who either stood or sat on the steps leading up to the entrance, this man was seated on some kind of throne-like ornate wooden chair. He had a thin, pale face and a thick moustache.

I leaned over to get a better look at the picture.

"It's him. It's the spook from the woods."

"Ernest Hoare Hales," Audrey said. "He was Holburn's first headmaster."

"Holy shit."

"There was a fire at the school in 1912. In the east wing. Everyone got out, but Ernest Hoare Hales died because he went back into the building to rescue a couple of girls who'd got trapped on the second floor. In the end they managed to find their own way out without his help. But he didn't come out again."

I clapped my hands together. "That's what you were shouting about out in the woods! The fire! You were telling him those girls got out! That's what got rid of him."

Audrey frowned. "You told me the best way to get rid of a ghost is to find out what it is that's keeping them here. I thought if he knew that everyone had escaped from that fire he could be at peace."

"You know what, Audrey, you're a frigging genius."

"You really think he's gone?"

I sat down on the desk. "You know, now that I think about it, when I was out in the woods with the priests, he only materialised when you joined us. How long have you been seeing him?"

"About a week or so. Since just before Ava and Lucy vanished."

"I'll bet Ava fastened him on to you."

"Fastened him on?"

"Made him watch over you."

"Do you think that branch broke because of him? Do you think he intended it to kill me?"

I shook my head. "No. He was gone by then. There was…"

"What?"

I recalled the small dark figure I'd seen. "There was another presence. I'm going back into the woods to find Ava."

Audrey gestured at the photograph album. "But what if he isn't gone? Something killed Father Stewart. I don't think it was just an accident. Maybe it was the same thing that killed Laura Fisher. It could be dangerous to go back out there."

"I'll have to take my chances. I can't wait any longer.

Ava's all alone in those woods now."

She moved her eyes the length of my body. "You better change first. You can't go anywhere like that. You'll catch you death."

I glanced towards the room's one small window, thinking of Ava all by herself in those woods. But I knew Audrey was right. I was soaked. And anyway, it was not yet noon. I had plenty of time left to look for Ava, there was no point heading out in wet clothes. And there was something else. I nodded to Audrey.

"I'll need that map."

Audrey waited in the refectory while I went to my room in the basement to change. Sensing Eve's spirit there, silent, watchful, I had to face the wall as I peeled off my wet clothes and pulled some dry ones from my overnight bag. In no time I was back upstairs and Audrey was leading the way to her own rooms in the staff quarters. There, I searched for some clue to her personality, but her rooms were functional: bed against one wall, dressing table, wardrobe, an armchair and an on-suit shower room. She had a few CDs—French Language tutorials and a couple of Leonard Cohen and Joni Mitchell albums. There was a watercolour painting of a vase of flowers which I guessed had come with the room, but aside from that the only framed picture was a photograph I took to be of the school staff. This picture stood on the dressing table. In it, the staff stood in the courtyard on the steps by the front entrance. Miss Inkson stood to one side of the group, poker-faced and with her usual air of authority. Audrey stood in the back row next to a tall grinning young man with wavy black hair. He was the only male in the group; no wonder he was grinning, sandwiched as he was between Audrey and a blonde woman, slightly older. On closer inspection, I realised it was the same man I'd encountered earlier that day leading the line of girls along the corridor.

"Who is that dude?" I said, indicating the picture.

"What?" Audrey had been looking through a pile of papers on the bed, trying to find the map we'd been using in the woods a few days earlier. She looked up.

"The man next to you in the photograph."

"Man? Oh. That… that's Gaspard."

Something in her tone made me what to know more.

"Who's Gaspard?"

"Gaspard Vassau. He teaches French here."

I didn't know why, but I had the impression I was tugging at the loose ends of a long story.

"You look very happy together." I pointed at the photograph. "At least we know someone can get a smile out of you."

I saw Audrey blush before she turned away and went on rifling through the papers on the bed.

"Were you two involved? Romantically?"

Audrey turned and flashed her eyes at me. "Why do you say that?"

"You got a bit flustered when I mentioned his name. You were involved, weren't you?"

"For a short while, yes. But I… I wasn't the only one."

"No?"

She pulled the map out from the loose sheets splayed across the bed and joined me by the dressing table. She pointed at the blonde woman in the photograph on Vassau's right.

"Who's that?"

"Miss Fisher. The music teacher."

"Ah," I said. I swallowed at the memory of the dead woman in the gymnasium. "I didn't recognise her."

"There were others too. A pupil. We all thought we were the only ones."

"A pupil? Wow. Gaspard, you dirty dog."

Audrey's face tightened in anger. "It's not funny. The girl — she killed herself."

I drew back and stared at her. "Over this guy?"

"He can be very charming. He could make you think…" She handed me the map.

"I'm amazed they let him carrying on teaching here."

"Oh, some of the parents wanted him fired. Especially Eve McArthur's. They…" She narrowed her eyes at me. "What's wrong?"

"Eve McArthur? Eve? She was the girl who killed herself? Over this French dude? You and Miss Fisher and Eve McArthur were in a love quadrangle with this guy?"

"I wouldn't put it quite like that, but yes. I suppose we were. Why? You know… something about her?"

"And this guy still teaches here?"

"They couldn't prove that Eve McArthur's suicide was his fault. Not directly. Or that anything had gone on between them. Eve was besotted with him, absolutely besotted, and I think he enjoyed the attention, but I don't know if he ever acted on it. It was just a rumour. Miss Inkson managed to keep it reasonably quiet, but there were ripples. I thought she'd make me give up my position, but she said it wasn't my fault. Said I'd fallen under his spell. But it wasn't quite like that, it… I…" She waved a hand. "Anyway, it damaged the school's reputation. That's why all this business with Ava and Miss Fisher's death has been so doubly terrible. We'd thought we were getting back on track."

"He hurt you, didn't he?" I took one of her hands in mine. She let me hold it a moment then removed it from my grasp.

"I brought it on myself. It was unprofessional."

"I think I'm starting to understand what's going on around here." In my mind's eyes I saw the body of Miss Fisher laid out in the school gymnasium, that awful look of terror frozen on her face that had been revealed when Father Bannister pulled back the covering sheet. And I remembered how something had tried to push Audrey into a ravine when we were walking in the woods, and how that branch had broken away from a tree and nearly killed her, hitting and killing Father Stewart instead. "I think you'd better lie low for a while, Audrey. Maybe you should leave here. Get away for a bit."

She looked stung. "Why do you say that?"

"Things are starting to make sense. I don't think that headmaster spook was ever a threat. Ava might have even had him watching over you as some kind of protector. I think there's an altogether different threat. A threat to you personally."

Fear showed on her face. Leaving me, she went into the shower room for a moment and returned rubbing at her hair with a towel. Seeing it loose and ruffled I had a strong urge to push my fingers into it. Audrey stopped rubbing at her head and looked at me, as if she'd known what I'd been thinking.

"I'm so sorry about your girlfriend," she said as she led me to the door. "It was horrible seeing you so upset yesterday."

"She wasn't my girlfriend anymore. She'd moved on. What would she want with a jerk like me, anyway? Someone who's always failing people. Kidding around. Shooting his mouth off. Letting people down."

"It wasn't your fault."

"Ah, I'm not so sure about that."

Stood in the door space, we faced each other.

"Gael," Audrey said. "The things that are happening here. I'm... I'm scared."

"Pack a bag," I said. "And go stay on the mainland for a few days. Until I've found Ava. Until I've sorted all this out."

"You really think I should?"

"I'm starting to think that's the best thing you could do right now."

"Take this," she said, placing her compass in my hand.

"Thanks," I said. "I'll trade you."

Reaching behind my head, I unfastened the clasp on my pendant. Then I reached around and placed it around Audrey's neck. As I fussed with the clasp, I could feel her breath on my face.

"What is this?" she said, lifting the crystal so that she could inspect it.

"Quartz. My mother gave it to me when I was fifteen or so."

"She gave this to you?"

"Yes. Things had got crazy in the house. I couldn't sleep."

"Crazy? What do you mean?"

I shook my head. "You don't want to know."

"Is this thing supposed to protect me?"

"That's the idea."

She glanced up. She smiled. "I never would've taken you for a man who believed in crystals."

"Yeah, well, me neither," I said, and stepped back into the hallway.

"Good luck," Audrey said. "I hope you find her."

I nodded, wanted to say something more but couldn't, then left.

Inkson collared me before I made it out of the staff quarters.

"Mr Drake," she said. "Can we talk?"

"I was just on my way out," I told her. "Can it wait?"

"Going to search for Ava, are you? You really think she's still out there in the woods?"

"If that Lucy girl was out there, then Ava has to be out there too. Has she come round by the way? Lucy? Has she said anything?"

"She's been ferried over to the mainland. The hospital there will keep us up to date with her progress. Mr Drake, I'd like to talk with you for a moment if you don't mind. In my, ah, in my rooms."

"Your rooms?"

"Yes."

"You mean your personal living quarters?"

She pursed her lips. "Yes. I'd... I'd like to get your opinion about something. A private matter."

"What kind of private matter?"

"Well, it's about my rooms. I don't want to make a fuss. Would you mind taking a look at them?"

I let out my breath. "You know that's a pretty cheap line, don't you, Miss Inkson?"

She looked mortified. "I..."

"Can't say I blame you though. My magnetism is pretty hard to resist."

His eyes filled my fury. "I don't mean *that*. Of course I don't mean *that*."

I suppressed a smirk. "What is it then?"

She took a deep shuddering breath to calm herself. "Maybe this was a bad idea."

Seeing how difficult she found it to ask for my help, I pitied her and put on my serious face. "I'm sorry. What's the problem?"

"Like I said, I don't want to make a fuss…"

"What is it? Spit it out."

"It's my rooms. These past few weeks…"

"Yes?"

"Well, I… I haven't felt entirely comfortable."

We traipsed back up to her rooms. I told myself to get this over with as quickly as possible. I was losing daylight. When we passed the closed door to Audrey's room I had a strong urge to knock. Just to see her face when she opened the door.

Stupid.

"Maybe I'm imagining it all," Inkson kept saying. Her rooms were at the very end of the corridor. "Maybe I'm cracking up. It wouldn't be much of a surprise with everything that's been going on at this school lately. What I've had to deal with."

"I'll be the judge of that," I said trying to lighten the

mood, but she only glared at me.

It surprised me how sparsely decorated her rooms were. Just like Audrey's. There was a short hallway with a bedroom immediately to the left and another door at the end which opened on to a long living room. The bedroom had a double bed, neatly made, and not much else. The living room was just as sparse as the bedroom. There were no pictures on the walls, no knick knacks scattered about the place. No shelf with books. No plant pots. Nothing.

"Very minimalistic," I said.

"I like my headspace uncluttered, Mr Drake."

"I get that."

Taking a deep breath, I tried to cast myself as some kind of professional ghost hunter, thinking that was what she wanted. "What exactly have you been experiencing here?"

"Noises. Sometimes. Like knocking. Footsteps. Scratching."

"Could be mice. You'd be surprised how loud they can be."

"One night a sound woke me and just for a split second I thought I saw a figure standing over me."

"That could've been a dream remnant. If you woke up suddenly, you could still have been seeing something from a dream. Like an afterimage."

She crossed her arms and stared at me. "I expected you to be a little more… receptive, Mr Drake."

I looked at her in surprise. "Wow. Never thought I'd hear you say that."

There were two doors leading off the living room. One led to a small kitchen: clean and sparkling, as if it had never been used. Back in the living room, I watched a shadow move across the walls all the way around the room until it reached the second door. I glanced at Miss Inkson, wondering if she'd seen it too.

I indicated the other door. "What's through there?"

"I use that room as an office."

"Can I go in?"

"Yes, but don't touch anything. Please."

I had not even got the office door open when a cold bolt of shock went through me. I wanted to shout, and it was all I could do to hold it in. For a moment I forgot myself and stood staring. Inside the room was a desk on which sat a computer, some stacks of paper, rolled up sheets and various bits of stationary. The desk chair stood to one side of the room, allowing me an unhindered view of what was underneath the desk. A pale thin figure was balled up there. I couldn't tell if it was male or female, as dark matted hair draped across one side of its face. It wore some kind of ragged and dirty-white dress or long t-shirt. The worst thing was that it glared straight back at me. I had never seen such a look of hatred on a person's face before.

Jesus Christ, Ava! Is there no end to this!

Where the hell had she got this one from?

Miss Inkson stood directly behind me, looking into the little office over my shoulder, and I felt sure she would have screamed if she saw the same thing I did. So why was I seeing it? Why just me? The ability to see spooks had always been confined to the women in my family. I looked again to be sure I wasn't imagining things.

The thing under the desk snarled at me and I took a step back. There was a terrible thick sense of malevolence that filled the entire space inside the room. Surely, I thought, Inkson felt this too? Doing my best to remain nonchalant, I continued backing out of the room and closed the door. I wasn't ready to face Miss Inkson yet, so I crossed to the window in the living room instead and looked out across the school grounds, looking for something mundane to reset my sense of the world.

Her window looked down on a small, gravelled area. There, a number of girls were seated on a concrete pew, huddled together and shivering. Before them, giving a lecture, stood my good buddy Gaspard, the French teacher. Seeing him, I felt the same bristle of dislike as I had the first time, only stronger now I knew the pain he'd caused Audrey.

This scene distracted me for only a moment. My thoughts quickly returned to the thing I'd seen under the desk in Inkson's little office. Ever since arriving at the school, I'd been telling myself Ava hadn't meant for anything bad to happen. She raised spooks because she was lonely. I didn't want to think her capable of a malicious act. But I could see no reason for her to have raised this particular horror other than to have it terrorise Miss Inkson.

Ava…? Jesus Christ. Why?

"Mr Drake? Is… everything all right?"

I was aware of Miss Inkson watching me from behind. I shook my head, hoping this would clear some of the shock from my face, before I turned to her. I didn't know what to say. Should I tell her? Would she believe me?

I turned to face her.

"You know," I said, choosing my words carefully. "Maybe you should get Father Bannister up here to do a little, you know…" I mimed scattering holy water.

"Why? What have you seen?" She half turned towards the closed door of the office.

"Nothing!" I swallowed hard. "Nothing. It couldn't hurt though, could it? Given what you've been experiencing?"

I could see she knew I was hiding something. Her face had blanched. Her eyes shifted again to the closed office door.

"Do it now," I said, hoping to convey a sense of urgency in my tone. "Right now."

She nodded. "Yes... yes I will, Mr Drake. I... thank you."

CHAPTER 7

As I set off on my trek, I couldn't stop thinking about those dreams I'd had the previous night: those people crowding around Ava in that basement room, and then holding Ava in my arms when she was a newborn baby and promising that I would protect her. What had happened to that promise? Ava had barely been out of nappies when I left my parents' house for good, tired of the madness, the strangeness, the voices, the shadows. I couldn't wait to escape from that house. I didn't feel protective towards Ava again until my parents' death when Carl had whisked her off to America. She'd written to me. I didn't even know she had my address. She told me how much she hated performing in Carl's stage shows. The things he had her do. For a shy girl like her, going up in front of a large theatre audience night after night must have been terrifying. But that was the least of it. She wrote that people would constantly find her backstage, and they would ask her about deceased mothers, husbands, children, friends. Plead with her to contact their dead loved ones. Thrusting photographs at her, or letters, or items of clothing. A child's bootee. A father's glove. A watch. It had become too much for her. All of it.

After receiving her letter, I flew to the US, and caught up with Carl's entourage in Chicago. He was performing at a place called The Cadillac Palace. Luckily for me, I'd played there the year before, when I'd replaced the lead guitarist for part of a tour in a punk rock outfit called Dead Batteries. The security guy remembered me. We'd smoked a few spliffs together after the Dead Batteries show. It surprised him to learn that I was Carl Drake's brother. I told him I'd flown over from Ireland to surprise Carl, and he let me go backstage. I snatched Ava during the first half of the show, while Carl was out on stage. I found her curled up in the dressing room. She burst into tears when she saw me. *Come on, Ava*, I said, *We're going home.* I told the security guy Ava was upset and needed some air. We stepped outside and just kept walking.

Musing on this led me to thinking about Elaine. *That's the last fucking time you walk out on me, Gael*, she'd said when she saw me packing for my trip to America. When I'd tried to explain that Ava needed me, she'd sneered: *Ava? When did you ever care about Ava? When did you ever care about anyone other than yourself, Gael Drake?*

Too harsh. I did what I could to help Ava. To save her. I couldn't ignore her letter. I couldn't pretend she was better off as some circus act. I had to help her. My mistake was not realising just how much help she'd needed.

Realising I was wondering aimlessly, lost in thought, I stopped and consulted the map and compass Audrey had given me. If I was going to find the stone lodge I had to be walking in a south-easterly direction. I corrected my course.

I began wondering about that pupil who'd killed herself over the handsome French teacher. Eve. I'd begun to think of her as my little spirit helper, but it seemed to me now that perhaps she was the malignant force at work in the school. She'd been besotted with Gaspard, Audrey had said. Absolutely besotted. So, she'd taken her own life, and Ava had brought her spirit back only to have it seek revenge on her love rivals. First Miss Fisher, then Audrey. Ava couldn't have anticipated that. It must have scared her. After the death of the music teacher, Ava must have put that head-teacher's ghost in place to watch over Audrey. Protect her. Somehow.

And that gruesome spook I'd seen under the desk in Inkson's office, how did that fit in? I did my best not to think about that. That would have to wait.

I hadn't been too long in the woods when I heard a voice call my name. Halting in my tracks, I flashed my gaze around the surrounding trees. Thinking I saw a movement behind a clutch of bushes a short distance away, I took a step towards them.

"Ava?"

I saw a flash of something dark then, and a female voice called, "Over here."

"Ava?"

Sharpening my gaze, I saw the bob of a dark head, moving away. I called my sister's name again and started running. After I'd passed the cluster of bushes where I'd seen the figure, I thought I saw something off about the ground ahead of me but I was moving so fast that by the time I realised this it was too late to stop. A loose array of broken branches and scattered leaves gave way underneath my weight and I found myself falling into a trench maybe three feet deep. I cried out with the pain of a twisted ankle.

With barely time to realise what had happened, I heard a flurry of footsteps in the undergrowth behind me and before I'd had a chance to turn around I was struck hard in the back of the head. The pain of it made my knees give out. Even as I fell forward, more blows suddenly began to rain down on me. They came from all sides, hitting me in the head and face, and in my arms and hands with which I tried to protect myself. Something struck me in the mouth and I tasted blood. As I tried to get away, I realised that the long trench I stood in looked more like a shallow grave. The sharp blows continued to pummel my head and shoulders with a speed and ferocity I couldn't believe. At one point my vision went blank, and I thought I was going to pass out, but then I came to my senses and bellowed with anger and began to swipe with my arms at whatever was hitting me. The onslaught stopped. I fell, panting against the side of the trench. I could feel a warm wet trickle running down one side of my face. I turned my head and spat blood. My head and shoulders and back were raw and aching from the volley of blows. Looking up, I saw a group of girls all wearing dark hooded shawls stood around the rim of the trench. They were breathing hard, and their faces were full of evil intentions. They were all holding hockey sticks, except for one tall, chunky girl who held a large heavy-looking log. I was certain that the log was going to be used to deliver the death blow, after which I realised with horror the girls would roll my body into this shallow grave I was already knelt in and cover me over.

I wiped a hand across my mouth. "What… what the fuck are you girls *doing*? What…?"

One girl stepped forward, her hockey stick poised for another whack at my skull. The hood covered her eyes, but seeing the birthmark on her cheek I recognised her as the girl I'd encountered on the stairway the day I'd arrived at the school. The one who'd looked at me with such hatred. And that day outside the classroom where the two priests were performing their exorcism. *Good luck finding your sister*, she'd said.

"You idiot," she said. "You shouldn't have had those priests exorcise the old headmaster."

"The headmaster? What're you…?"

"The man in the black suit. Ava put him here to protect Hendy."

So, I'd been right.

"Protect Hendy? Audrey, you mean? Protect her from who?"

"From who do you think? From the dead girl."

"The dead girl? You… what… what dead girl?"

"The French teacher was screwing them all. Hendy, Fisher, and Eve. Eve killed herself over him, but then your bloody sister went and dragged her up again. Eve was her only friend for a while. But Eve was still nuts over the French teacher. That's why she went after Fisher. Now the headmaster's ghost is gone, she'll go after Hendy too."

"What? Audrey…?"

I saw what she meant suddenly. Eve was the dead girl. Eve, the girl who'd killed herself over Gaspard Vassau. My suspicions were confirmed. That little love quadrangle was still playing itself out. It was Eve's ghost that had killed the music teacher, Miss Fisher, Eve's ghost that had tried to push Audrey into the ravine that day in the woods. Eve's ghost that had made a tree branch fall and kill Father Stewart. And the man in the black suit? Could it be true? Had Ava put him here to protect Audrey? But now he was gone, exorcised, and now Eve was free to…

The birthmark girl jabbed at my face with her hockey stick. "You never should have come here. We don't want you here. Freaks like you and your sister. You never should have brought her here."

As she talked I tried to crawl backwards out of the trench. I already knew that I had no chance of making a run for it on my damaged ankle. So this was it then? This was the way I went out. Battered to death by a bunch of hockey stick wielding schoolgirls. It wasn't the ending I'd envisioned for myself, that was for sure. When the girls closed in around me, I threw out both hands.

"Wait! Wait! What the fuck do you think you're doing? What are you doing, girls? Eh? Eh? What is this? What is it?"

"We're helping you find your freak show sister. That's what you want, isn't it? To find her."

"What? What the hell do you mean?" But I was starting to understand. "You didn't hurt Ava did you, girls? Tell me you didn't hurt Ava."

"We did more than hurt her," birthmark said. "You don't understand. That freak didn't belong here. We all had to share a dorm with her. We'd had enough. She was unnatural. The things she could do. She was evil. Unnatural."

Elaine's voice in my head again. *Unnatural. It's unnatural, Gael, what she can do.*

"And so she had to be put down."

I gasped. "Put... put down?"

Without me realising it, the tall girl had moved around the back of the others so that she stood behind me. I felt the log she carried strike the back of my head with a sickening thud and my world went black. A sudden flurry of movement and a chorus of screams followed me down into the dark.

CHAPTER 8

When I opened my eyes, I was in that windowless basement room again, the one from the dream I'd had where Ava sat at a table in the centre, and all those people — those dead people — had crowded around her. Same bare concrete walls. Same stark light from a single light-bulb dangling from the ceiling. Only this time there was no table, and no Ava. I was the one occupying the centre of the room, and stood a few inches away and facing me was a girl of about fifteen or sixteen years old. She wore the Holburn Academy uniform. I recognised the crest on the breast pocket of her blazer as that of the school. It was a shield that had been split into three sections. In the lower section there was a symbol of an open book. In the left-hand section above was a heart pierced by two arrows. And on the right there was what could have been a lion or a dragon.

The girl's strawberry blonde hair was matted and dishevelled, and there was a smell off her. A smell of dirt. Or earth. She had her head tilted to one side as she looked up at me, and she was grinning. At the same time, she fixed me with an intense, unblinking stare. Her eyes were big dark pools. I was aware that there were other people in the room, stood pressed against the walls. I could see them in my peripheral vision. But I could not look their way, so forcibly did the eyes of the girl stood before me hold on to mine. Something in her face reminded me of a crazed fan who'd followed around an ex-boy band singer I'd toured with once, always appearing in the front row of every concert he played, always trying to get back stage.

What's the problem? I'd teased him once after he'd pointed her out. *She's cute.*

Cute, but unhinged, he'd told me, annoyed that I'd made a joke of it. *Seriously, that girl does* not *get backstage. I'm not joking. She's got crazy in her eyes. Who knows what she might be capable of?*

When the same girl accosted me outside the stage door after a show, I saw exactly what he meant.

The girl facing me there in that basement room startled me then by laughing heartily, letting her head fall back. Seeing my alarm made her laugh even more.

"We've been waiting for you," she said. "What took you so long?"

I gave a cursory glance around the room. "Where am I?"

"Shall we dance?" the girl said. Before I could protest, she clutched one of my hands in one of hers, fastened her other hand on my waist, and using a strength a girl of her size should not have possessed, she forced me to lurch with her around the room in an awkward tango. As there was no music she began to hum. *Da-da-dar da-da-dar da-dar da-da-dar da-da-dar da-dar.* She upped the tempo as she spun me in frantic circles. However much I tried, I found I couldn't break away from her.

I'm not joking. She's got crazy in her eyes. Who knows what she might be capable of?

"Help," I said, to the people stood against the walls. "Help me."

Turning my head to left and right as the girl span me around, I saw now who the people were stood propped against the walls, watching us with impassive faces. They were all here: Ernest Hoare Hales, Miss Fisher, Father Stewart, Elaine, even my parents. I called out to them again as the girl, laughing, whirled me around the centre of the room. She was still humming. *Da-da-dar da-da-dar da-dar da-da-dar da-da-dar da-dar.* When I stumbled and fell onto one knee, she didn't release me. She held on fast. She spun me around again as soon as I was back on me feet. The others in the room continued to watch, mute and blank-faced.

I'd not realised the room had a door in one wall until it burst open so forcefully that it crashed against the inside wall.

"Eve!" a voice commanded. "Stop!"

I looked into the face of my dancing partner. So this was Eve. All the mirth fled from her features. She stopped spinning me around and scowled over my shoulder. Following her gaze I saw another girl of similar age stood in the open doorway. A bright light from behind silhouetted her, so I couldn't make out her face. Not until she spoke again did I realise it was my sister, Ava.

"Leave him alone," Ava said. I had never known her to use such a strident tone.

"No way!" Eve shot back. She gripped my hand tighter, crushing it so hard I began to moan. "I won't! He's ours now."

"No he isn't."

Ava strode forward, and I watched in amazement as she wrenched Eve's hands away from me and threw her to the floor. Eve crabbed backwards, glaring up at me and Ava. Then Ava took my hand in hers.

"Come on, Gael," she said. "I'm taking you home."

She led me to the door. There was a short passageway with steps leading upwards. From the top of the steps came a dazzling light which hurt my eyes. I had to shield my face with one hand as Ava drew me up the steps. Halfway up she let go of my hand and urged me to continue alone. It was then that I heard a different voice, a man's voice, a voice I thought I knew, repeating my name. I climbed the steps towards it.

CHAPTER 9

"Gael? Gael?"

I opened my eyes, squinting against needles of sunlight. Someone was lightly slapping the side of my face.

"Gael? Gael?"

I lay on my back in a pile of dead leaves.

The girls hadn't finished me off, nor dragged me into the grave and buried me — if indeed that had been their intention, it seemed difficult to believe. My vision swam. A blurry figure hovered above me. Attempting to raise myself, I blinked at stars exploding before my eyes. One side of my face felt swollen, and I had sharp agonising pains in my head, neck and shoulders.

"You've taken quite a beating," the man's voice said. "What the hell happened to you?"

With one hand I attempted to shield my eyes.

"Who is that?"

"Don't you recognise your own brother, Gael? It's me. Carl."

I stiffened and drew back. When my vision cleared, I saw that it was true. Carl was crouched above me. His face had filled out some since the last time I'd seen him, and his hair and goatee beard was now a shade of orangey-red that screamed 'dye-job'. He wore a black shirt and trousers with a long black leather jacket over the top. When he smiled at me, his teeth were startlingly white. Looking down at me over his shoulder was a slim blonde wearing a pant-suit and sunglasses.

"What... Carl... what're you doing out here?"

"I came as soon as I heard," he said. His Irish accent had been flattened-out and his voice now had an Americanised twang. "To help find Ava. The school principal's assistant told me you'd gone wandering about by yourself in the woods, so I came to see if I could find you."

"School principal's assistant? You mean Audrey? Audrey's still here. I told her to leave."

"She was the one who met us when we arrived."

I looked around frantically. "Where're the girls?"

"Girls?"

"The girls who attacked me. Didn't you see them?"

"I haven't seen anyone." He gestured at the woman behind him. "Valerie and I have been wandering about in these woods for almost an hour looking for you. We were about to throw in the towel, but then Valerie saw an arm sticking out of this hole here."

I tried to lift myself but couldn't. "They tried to fucking kill me. They wanted to kill me and bury me in this hole. Make me disappear."

"Who did?"

"I don't know — a bunch of girls."

"You don't mean to say some of the girls from the school attacked you?"

Seeing him smirk, I yelled at him. "That's exactly what I fucking mean!"

Blood mixed with drool flew from my mouth. Carl drew back.

I sat up, wincing at the pain in my head. Why wasn't I dead? I remembered the screams I'd heard before I'd blacked out. Maybe something had scared them away. Remembering then what the birthmark girl had said about Ava, I felt my stomach contract and I hunched forward and vomited. Tears stung my eyes. Could it be true? Had those girls lured Ava out into these woods and killed her? Beaten her to death with hockey sticks and dumped her in a shallow grave just like the one I was sitting in? I already knew they were capable of it — they'd tried to do the exact same thing to me, hadn't they? Had they meant to kill Lucy too? Had Lucy managed to escape them somehow, escape into the woods and hide there?

Jesus Christ.

Carl rose to his feet. "We'd better get you back to the school and cleaned up, Gael. Then we can start thinking about how we're going to track Ava down. That was quite a stunt you pulled in Chicago. You made a real bags of my career for a while there. I had to cancel the rest of the tour, you know, and refund all the tickets. You cost me an absolute fortune, you eejit, and I'm not about to forget it. Come on, get up. So where do we think Ava's hiding?"

I looked straight at him and shook my head. "It's no use, Carl. It's no use. I don't think we're going to find Ava. Not alive."

His face dropped.

"What are you talking about? I need her, Gael."

"You callous bastard," I said. "I tell you that you're baby sister might be dead, and all you can think about is your fucking career. You always were a shit, Carl. A total fucking shit. Help me up."

It was then that I remembered something else that birthmark girl had said.

The man in the black suit. Ava put him here to protect Hendy.

Protect Hendy? From who?

Who do you think? From the dead girl.

I clutched at Carl now, trying desperately to get to my feet. Pain screamed in my ankle. All I could think about was Audrey. I had to save her. If I couldn't save Ava and I couldn't save Elaine, then I was going to fucking save someone.

"Take it easy," Carl said.

"No, we have to get back. There's a woman there. Back at the school. Audrey. She's in danger."

Carl motioned his companion forwards so that the two of them could help me out of the hole. As he lifted me gingerly, probably worried about getting blood on his expensive-looking shirt, he looked me squarely in the face.

"You really think Ava's dead?"

"Go fuck yourself, Carl."

Attempting to lead Carl and Valerie, or whatever her name was, back to the school, I realised again what a beating I'd taken. I could barely walk. I'd only gone a few paces when I had to stop and rest against a tree. There were dozens of aches and pains all over my body. Tiny lights erupted before my eyes. I couldn't make a fist with my left hand either. There was a good chance I'd never play guitar again. Carl stood watching me, looking baffled. Valerie gazed deeper into the woods.

"Are you telling me you think Ava might be dead?" Carl said again.

I squeezed my eyes tight shut. I didn't want to think about that. Not now. It was too horrible to contemplate. I had to save Audrey.

"There's a lot of crazy shit going on here on this island, Carl. I'd fill you in, but right now we need to get back to the school."

As I started forward, I felt my head spin and lurched to the side.

"Let me help you," Carl said, full of belated concern.

I slung one arm around his shoulder and limped as best I could. Valerie led the way. We arrived back at the school in time to see girls flooding out of the back door into the rear garden. They looked terror stricken and stared at me in horror as Carl, Valerie and I made our way through them.

"What's going on?" I said to one group, but they closed ranks and drew away from us.

There was a crash of breaking glass and looking up I saw something sailing out from one of the school's second-floor windows. Screams went up from the groups of girls, and they moved en masse towards the far end of the lawn. Whatever had shot out from the top window landed with a splintering sound on the steps leading to the rear entrance. On reaching it, I saw that it was the framed photo of the school staff I'd earlier looked at in Audrey's room. Hearing a scream, I looked up at the broken window.

"Audrey!"

"What the beejesus is going on?" Carl said.

"We have to help her."

Ignoring my various aches and pains, I broke away from Carl, lurched up the steps, and entered the school. The ground floor appeared deserted, but I could hear a commotion from somewhere above. Struggling up the steps, I caught my reflection in a mirror mounted on the wall at a turn in the staircase. There was a large swelling above my right eye, goo matted my hair, and a gash on my forehead still oozed blood down the left side of my face. I thought of those girls who had done this to me. Birthmark and her pals. Those little fucking psychos. I would find them all later, I told myself, and I would make sure they paid.

CHAPTER 10

A group of people clustered together on the second-floor landing, outside Audrey's rooms. Hadlee was there with a few of his constables, as was Father Bannister. Inkson was there too, with some other people who I took to be employees of the school. It was Inkson who first noticed me as I stumbled down the hall trailing Carl and Valerie. Her face opened in shock. I don't think she even recognised me until I spoke.

"What's going on? Where's Audrey?"

Still staring in horror at my face, she pointed with one trembling hard towards the door the group clustered around. "She's... we can't..."

Pushing past her, I caught Hadlee by the arm and span him to face me. He too did a double-take.

"What's going on?"

"There's something going on inside Miss Hendy's room. We can't open the door."

"Break the damn thing down."

"We've tried. It appears to be wedged from inside."

I forced my way closer to the door. I shouted Audrey's name, but was answered only by a scream and the sound a glass shattering. Something slammed hard against the wall to one side of the door. I directed my plea at the dead girl.

"Eve!" I shouted, as loudly as I could. The noises inside the room ceased. "Eve! Don't do this. Leave her alone. She's not to blame for what happened. Open this door!"

I tried the door handle, but it still wouldn't budge.

"Eve! You said you wanted to help me, remember? Let us in."

I put my ear to the door, just as something crashed against it from the other side, making me reel back. I heard Audrey scream again.

"Eve! No! This is wrong!"

Hadlee's voice from behind me: "Who the hell are you talking to, man? Who's Eve?"

Ignoring him, I looked around for Carl, saw him talking to Inkson, and grabbed onto his coat.

"We need to get Ava here."

"What?"

"We need to summon Ava. She's the only one who can put this right."

"Summon her? What the hell are you talking about?"

"Look, I know you're a fraud, Carl, and it was Ava who did the summoning in your show, okay; but she's your sister so if you give it a go, it might just work this time. Okay?"

"Gael, I can't just... anyway, we don't know Ava's dead. She might still be..."

"I know."

There was a loud crash from inside Audrey's room, followed by another scream. Then I heard Audrey shouting at someone to leave her alone.

"Oh Christ," I said, "if we don't do something fast Audrey's going to end up like that music teacher." I looked at Inkson. "You want another body in your gymnasium?"

"What's all this talk about Ava being dead?" Inkson said. "She's not dead. She's out there somewhere in those woods."

I shook my head. "No. No, she isn't. She's lying in a

shallow grave somewhere. Some of the other girls here murdered her."

Inkson's eyes bulged and mouth fell open. "What? How... what are you implying?"

My anger got the better of me then. "I'm not *implying* anything. I'm telling you — a group of girls from this school killed my sister. They tried to kill that Lucy girl, and then they tried to beat me to death with their bloody hockey sticks. Look at me! I didn't get like this from walking into a fucking doorpost, did I!"

Carl took a firm hold on my arm then and led me a short distance away from the group. Looking me in the eye, and speaking in a low voice, he said, "Gael. You're talking crazy. Why don't we just calm down, okay?"

I brushed him off. "Listen to me, Carl. When Ava first came here, she was so lonely she pulled the spook of a dead girl out of the wall. They were a gang — Ava, Lucy and Eve — that's the dead girl's name. Eve killed herself over some affair she had with her French teacher. That French teacher also had a fling with the music teacher, who's now dead, and Audrey, the woman inside that room. Don't you see? There's a spirit in there that's mad as hell. It's already killed one woman, and soon it's going to kill another. Ava put another spook here to protect Audrey, but I didn't know. I made the priests get rid of it. Now Eve can do whatever she wants, and Ava's the only one who can stop her."

Carl held my gaze for a long moment. "I can't bring Ava here, Gael. You know I can't."

"Try, for fuck's sake. *Try*."

Father Bannister, with Miss Inkson at his shoulder, emerged from the group clustered around Audrey's door. Grabbing hold of my arm, and sending pain shooting up into my shoulder, he turned me to face him.

"For Heaven's sake, what's going on here, boy?" He looked me up and down. "What happened to you? You look like you were hit by a truck."

Before I could say anything, Carl tried to intervene, but I pushed him away.

"Get your holy water and your Bibles out Father," I said. "We've got another spook to banish."

Bannister's eyes lit. "Where is it?"

"Where do you think it is? In that room with Audrey. It's trying to kill her."

He didn't need further encouragement, and I had to commend him for that. Bannister turned back towards the door to Audrey's room and bellowed, "Make way! Make way!" in a voice so commanding that a path opened up in the crowd of people clustered in the hallway. Bannister went forward. Out came the holy water and the Bible. He began to recite in Latin, at the same time making the sign of the cross and splashing holy water over Audrey's door. Some of the people gathered turned dumbfounded gazes on me, as if for an explanation of what they were witnessing. Before long I was flat up against the wall listening. On the other side of the wall, inside Audrey's room, it had fallen silent. I was just about to urge the priest on when the door to Audrey's room shook within its frame. All of us gathered there saw it. Father Bannister took a cautionary step back just as the door burst open so violently, that it crashed against the outside wall. I heard Inkson utter a low moan, but everyone else was silent, waiting to see who or what would emerge from the room. Nothing did though, apart for a great rush of air which threw Father Bannister backwards into the throng. Hadlee and a few of his men went down like bowling pins. Then a terror-struck Father Bannister was lifted into the air and flung hard against the wall at the opposite end of the corridor. He bounced off the wall and slammed across the bannister at the top of the stairwell. I felt for him, but as he crumpled to the floor, the door to Audrey's room slammed shut again — apparently of its own accord — and when a brave copper stepped forward and tried to yank it open, he couldn't.

I caught Inkson's eye then. She looked frantic. "What was that?" she said, looking at me and flailing her arms. She gestured at the prone figure of Father Bannister. He lay face down on the floor, groaning and trying to raise himself. "What was it?"

Others in the group where clustered around the priest, trying to lift him into a sitting position. Hadlee sat propped against the wall, looking dazed.

I looked around for Carl and saw him making for the stairs with Valerie scurrying at his heels.

I called his name, but he didn't look back.

"You bloody coward," I shouted after him. "You bloody useless coward!"

He stopped at the foot of the stairs and turned to look back at me. "You've made a real mess of things, Gael. You should have left Ava with me. All this is your fault. It's beyond my powers to interfere. And the truth is, I don't want any part in it. I'm sorry."

With that he and Valerie went running off towards the school's main doors.

I turned back to the door to Audrey's room, attempting to focus my thoughts.

Eve's too strong, I realised. *She's too strong for any of us. Bibles and holy water is not the way.* My thoughts returned to that morning in the woods when we had banished the headmaster's ghost. I remembered that it was not the priests who'd dispelled him, but Audrey telling him about those girls he'd tried to rescue from a fire, and how they'd got out unharmed.

You told me the best way to get rid of a ghost is to find out what's keeping them here, I remembered her saying. *I thought if he knew everyone had escaped from that fire he could be at peace.*

What's keeping them here?

What was keeping Eve here?

I glanced towards the staircase then, and that's when I saw him. He stood on the highest step, looking back at me.

"Gaspard!"

Hearing me say his name, he retreated down the staircase. I signalled to one of the policemen.

"Get him. Get him over here. He's the one that can put an end to this."

The policeman looked puzzled, so I said with greater emphasis, gesturing wildly at the figure hurrying down the staircase: "Get him! Get the French teacher! Bring him here!"

The policeman glanced at Hadlee, who gave a nod of ascent, then nudged one of his colleagues. The two of them rushed after Gaspard. A few moments later they returned, leading the stricken-faced man ahead of them.

"Stand him in front of the door," I said.

"This is nothing to do with me!" Gaspard said, looking around the assembled with wild eyes.

"Stand him in front of the door."

The policeman blocked his retreat, so seeing that he had no choice, Gaspard moved though the throng and stood before the door to Audrey's room.

He glared at me. "Now what?"

"Call out to Eve McArthur."

His face tightened. "Eve McArthur? That girl is dead."

"Call out to Eve McArthur," I said. "Just do it."

He gave me a black look then faced the door. Drawing a deep breath he said, "Eve McArthur."

"Louder."

"Eve McArthur!"

The noise inside the room continued.

"Louder," I told him. "Louder!"

"Eve McArthur!" Gaspard said. He shouted it. "Eve, it's me! Gaspard!"

The noises inside Audrey's room ceased.

Gaspard blanched. He threw me a pleading look.

"Ask her if you can come in."

"What?"

"Ask her if you can come in."

"Are you kidding me? I will not go inside that room. Merde Alors!"

"Audrey Hendry's life's in danger," I reminded him. "Ask Eve if you can come into the room."

He held my gaze for a moment. Then, again drawing a deep breath, he said, "Eve? Eve, may I come in?" His voice had a quaver in it.

At once the door to the room swung inward. At this, Gaspard tried to make a break for it, but I saw what he intended and leapt forward to grab hold of his arm. Though the pains in my body screamed, I summoned the strength to push him into the room.

"Tell her you're sorry!" I called, before the door slammed shut again.

There was a long silence inside the room. Listening intently, I heard Gaspard talking in a low voice which quickly turned to a shout, and then a holler.

There was a terrible commotion from inside Audrey's room, followed by a furious prolonged thwarted scream, so loud that some of those assembled pressed their hands over their years. I began pushing my way back through the group, and as I reached the door to Audrey's room it sprang open before me. I looked inside. The room was in disarray. It barely resembled the room I'd stood in earlier. It was as if a cyclone had blown through it. The bed had been reduced to splinters, the mattress torn open, and the stuffing dragged out and strewn around the floor. The armchair stood upturned and buckled against one wall. The dressing table was in pieces. The wardrobe doors had been torn off their hinges and the clothes inside reduced to rags. The window was smashed and the walls at various points looked like a great iron fist had punched holes in them.

"Sweet Mary Mother of God," I heard Hadlee say as he entered the room at my back.

At first I didn't see Gaspard anywhere in the room. In my mind's eyes I pictured him and Eve McArthur locked together in a lover's embrace as she drew him with her into whatever black purgatorial depths Ava had dragged her out of. But then I saw him slumped against the wall behind the door. His eyes were wide and staring, and he was shaking his head and saying under his breath, "No no no no no. No no no no no."

"Hey," I said. But he didn't seem to see me. "Hey, Gaspard. You okay?"

Nothing. He went on mumbling to himself. Hadlee and a couple of others tried to get him on to his feet.

I began desperately looking around for Audrey, sure that she at least had to be here somewhere. I couldn't see her anywhere. Then I remembered about the small on-suite bathroom. The door was closed, although it was dented in the centre as if a bull had charged at it. I went to it and tried the knob. It wouldn't open. I hammered my fist against the wood.

"Audrey. It's all right. She's gone now. You can come out. Audrey? Audrey?"

For a long moment, I heard nothing from the other side of the door. Then there was a great wrenching sob, and I let out my breath in relief. I turned to the crowd clustered in the doorway.

"She's alive," I said. "It's all right. She's alive."

The bathroom door opened, and I saw Audrey crouched on the floor behind it. She stared up at me with wide fear-filled eyes. She was in such a bad way that I almost didn't recognise her. In her two hands she clutched something tight. Seeing the broken cord trailing from her closed fists, I realised it had to be my crystal quartz pendant.

"Audrey," I said. "It's over. It's all over."

EPILOGUE

Climbing out of the bed, I crossed to the window. The view looked out over the harbour and the steely grey water beyond. From here the sea looked calm. I recalled the rough crossing of the previous week, when I first went out to The Holburn Academy. I should have taken that as a sign. I should have known then that I was in for a turbulent time.

Opening the door, and stepping out into the corridor, I paused. The strip lights flickered. A figure stood in the half-dark at the far end of the corridor, looking back at me. Her face was hidden inside the hollow of her hood. I lifted a hand to reach out to her. I wanted to take her up in my arms and hold her, just as I had when she was a baby. But I knew this wasn't flesh and blood Ava. It was only a spirit. Something flashed in my memory, and I realised this wasn't the first time I'd seen her. The day I arrived at the school, when Inkson had taken us out to the edge of the woods to show us the spot where the music teacher's body was found, I'd glanced back towards the school building and had seen a girl stood in the rain watching us. I realised then it was Ava I'd seen. And that same figure I'd glimpsed when I was led out into the garden and found Lucy. I'd thought it was Eve, but that too had been Ava. She'd been with me all along.

She looked back at me with her brow lowered. She had the sulky expression on her face she'd sometimes worn during that time when she'd stayed with Elaine and me, when I'd lectured her or told her off about something. The expression she wore when she knew she'd done something wrong.

"Ava," I said. "I'm sorry. I'm sorry I didn't try harder. I'm sorry I let this happen to you."

I blinked and she was gone, vanished, and something told me she wouldn't be back. That she was at peace. I walked along the corridor to a room a few doors down from mine. The door stood open.

"Knock knock," I said.

Audrey lifted her head from the pillows and gave a wan smile. I took this as a welcome and entered, sitting down in the chair next to her bed. One of her eyes was still swollen shut and she had a row of stitches across her forehead. There was a cast on her lower left arm. Her other arm had scratch marks on it which began near the shoulder and reached all the way down to her wrist.

She turned her face to me. "How do I look?"

Reaching forward, I patted her hand. "You're alive. That's the main thing."

"She wanted to kill me, didn't she?"

I shrugged. Nodded.

She uttered a brittle little laugh then. "All because of Gaspard. It's unbelievable."

"He must have been one hell of a charmer."

"What happened to him?"

"I heard he's gone back to France. I don't know what Eve did to him, or showed him, but I doubt he'll ever get over it."

She met my eyes again. I could see from the look in them that she was still having a hard time believing what had happened. I couldn't blame her. I was still struggling with it myself, and I'd been seeing and hearing ghosts for as long as I could remember.

"I'm sorry," Audrey said. "About Ava. If it's true, I'm…"

"The police are searching the woods behind the school. At last." I paused. Swallowed. Looked around for something to drink. "For her body I mean. They say they can't arrest anyone until they find a body, even though both me and Lucy What's-her-name have given a statement."

"Lucy Devonshire-Bartram."

"That's what I said."

Her eyes narrowed. "And your brother? What was his name? Carl?"

"He got the fright of his life, and took off out of there."

Audrey smiled. She shook her head, and took a deep breath. "So, what now, Gael? What happens now?"

I leant forward again and took her hand in mine. "The good news is the doctor's say I might never play guitar again. I won't make a living as a jobbing muso anymore. And I'll never be Jimi Hendrix. So, I'll have to find something else to do with my life."

Audrey looked hard at me. "That's good news?"

I squeezed her hand. "It might just be."

About the Author

Tim Jeffreys' short fiction has appeared in Supernatural Tales, Not One of Us, The Alchemy Press Book of Horrors 2 & 3, Stories We Tell After Midnight 2 & 3, Nightscript, and many other publications too numerous to list here. His co-written science fiction novella, Voids, was published by Omnium Gatherum in 2016. He hails from the north of England, but now lives in Bristol with his partner and two children. He is currently at work on several novels. Follow his writerly progress at www.timjeffreys.blogspot.co.uk.

Previous Works

Black Masquerades
(short story collection)

You Will Never Lose Me
(short story collection)

Voids
(novella, co-written with Martin Greaves)